SEEKING THE
HIGH YELLOW
NOTE

To carol,
with the hope that
you'll be inspired in
your painting by
Vincents story.
        Alice Heard William

14850-WILL

SEEKING THE HIGH YELLOW NOTE

Vincent Van Gogh in Provence,
A Novel

Alice Heard Williams

This is a work of fiction. Names, characters, places and incidents either are the product of the author's imagination or are used fictitiously, and any resemblance to any actual persons, living or dead, events, or locales is entirely coincidental.

This book was printed in the United States of America.

To order additional copies of this book, contact:
Xlibris Corporation
1-888-795-4274
www.Xlibris.com
Orders@Xlibris.com

For James

CHAPTER ONE

In 1986, under modest headings, the following brief item appeared in many newspapers around the world: Madame Minette Ginoux Martin died Thursday, June 8, in the Provencal city of Arles where she had lived many of her 116 years. Madame Martin retained all of her faculties until her death, clearly recalling events of her life in a memoir written a few years earlier. In 1888 she met the artist Vincent Van Gogh, who had recently arrived from Paris and remained in Arles for 15 months, considered by art experts to be the most productive period of his short life.

*   *   *

Yes, I met Vincent when I was only sixteen, a slip of a girl recently arrived in Arles from Saint Remy after a great tragedy in my family. Odd, isn't it, I came from the town where Vincent went later to be cured. Ha! I could have told anyone who would listen: they created lunatics at that hospital in Saint Remy. No one left that hospital sane! Vincent left it with a thousand devils chasing around in his head, clamoring to be let out. Yes, I knew Vincent Van Gogh. My memories of him are as clear as though it were yesterday.

I arrived in Arles in sadness, forced to leave my home when my father was killed in an accident. He was trampled to death by a rampaging ox as he struggled to lead the beast to drink at a stream running alongside the olive grove where he had been collecting the old, dead wood to burn.

My mother accepted his death with a stoicism which I could not understand. To me it was an outrage: a man in the prime of his life struck down, leaving a wife and five children without means of support. It meant I would have to go to Arles to work. This is how it came about.

Surely it was God's will and not her place to question, my mother believed. A quiet, reserved woman with quick, energetic movements, deeply-set gray eyes, a straight nose, she only knew in her numbing grief she had lost her beloved husband and had five children to feed. Her face had been pretty once, her small mouth full and rosy, but time and hard labor in the fields beside my father had erased her beautiful features as surely as a sponge wipes clean a slate.

As the oldest child, I understood her fears. I had been helping in the fields for two years, leaving school which I had loved, at fourteen. These thoughts and grief for my father placed a great weight on my chest as I lay sleepless in the narrow bed under the eaves the evening after the funeral mass.

There were few mourners at the burial. My father's only brother had died some years ago. His widow Marguerite, my aunt Titi, came from Arles where she managed the restaurant my uncle had started. Aunt Titi had a beautiful, expressive face, a sharp nose with piercing brown eyes that could grow warm and kind, lustrous black hair bound tightly to her head. She wore her clothing like an empress, white fichu, or neckpiece, arching majestically over an ample bosom, the black wool dress giving a *cachet*, a presence to her full figure.

I could hear her whispering with my mother long into the night as they lay beside each other in the old bed where together my mother and father had lain all their married life. Up in the loft, surrounded by my brothers and sisters whose breathing as they lay on their pallets sounded like a basket of purring kittens, I strained to hear what the women were saying below, but I could not. Only the sharp intonations of my aunt's singsong voice mingling with the softer murmurs of my mother wafted up to my ears, the words themselves indistinct.

It was not long until I found out what the whisperings were about. Breakfast the next morning finished quickly. It takes only a matter of a few minutes for five children and two adults to drink cups of black coffee and chew slices of leftover bread. Hungrily my brother Paul eyed the end of the loaf in front of my mother as she cut off another slice for Aunt Titi. My aunt's gaze fixed on Paul, his small face dwarfed by huge, hungry eyes, and she silently handed over the bread to him. He stuffed it in his mouth before my mother could object.

"Paul, do you not know to thank someone who does you a kindness?" she asked mildly.

"*Merci, Tante Titi,*" he mumbled, his mouth working in the most disgusting way, jammed full of bread.

"It is of no importance," Aunt said, patting his head. "He is a good boy."

I glowered at Paul who had the grace to lower his eyes. All of us were hungry, and as one of the older children, he should have behaved better, I thought resentfully. My mother turned to me and spoke.

"Minette, pack your things now that you have finished breakfast. I'll clean up here."

Dumbfounded, I looked into her eyes, the region around my heart turning to ice.

"You will be going back to Arles with Titi. She can use more help at the cafe, and you will send back your wages each week to help out here. Now Paul and Roger will go to the fields with me. Colette and Francine will stay at the house and do the laundry for our customers as they have been taught to do. I'll do the ironing in the evenings."

My mother calmly voiced her carefully planned litany. I knew she was gambling on our unquestioning loyalty even though at that moment my heart was quietly breaking. How could I possibly leave home so soon after my father's death? Our house and our lives were humble, it is true, but bound together with love and kindness. Now everything was tumbling down around me like a collapsing house of cards. I did not want to leave. But I could say nothing. To speak I knew would unleash the tears behind my mother's eyes and sweep us all away on a current of weeping and helplessness.

As we sat around the old table in that downstairs room I looked at my aunt. She kept her eyes lowered. I could not guess her thoughts. But I knew instinctively it was her plan we were adopting, and I realized she was doing us a great kindness.

It was the work of a few minutes to gather up my belongings, tying them loosely into the black shawl that sheltered me from the cold and rain in Provencal winters. I looked one last time around the room then went slowly down the stairs like a prisoner going to his execution. I thought of the many meals we had shared at the old table. But with Father gone, it will never be the same, an angry voice inside me cried. Never the same.

My aunt stood ready at the door with my mother, whose hands fidgeted with her white apron, her black dress billowing awkwardly about her. She was more at home in the brown homespun she wore to the fields than in her Sunday dress. Paul and Roger stared unblinking, while Colette and Francine, ranged on either side of me, reacted in sharply different ways. Colette tossed her black curls saucily and smiled like a cat in the cream jug. She would inherit my bed. No longer would she sleep on a pallet on the hard floor. Francine, tender-hearted, wept soundlessly, tears streaming down her cheeks. She could not take in the enormity of all which had happened. She only realized that her little world had suddenly fallen to pieces around her, like a broken *poupon*, or doll. But there would be few thoughts about dolls in my head now. Overnight it seemed I had grown up. Quickly I hugged her, then pressed against my mother, my head nestling down, resting on her neck.

"*Maman, Maman!*" I did not trust myself to say more. "Go with God, Minette," she whispered in my ear and hugged me tightly, the pain showing in her gray eyes. "There is no other way." Her voice trembled. We climbed on the wagon belonging to the farmer who had brought my aunt from Arles. In a few seconds I could barely see our house beside the road. The figures of my mother, my brothers and sisters were as tiny specks of black earth in the distance.

*   *   *

February is a cruel month in the Midi, our part of Provence, and my first days in Arles were tempered by a miserable gray snow which refused to melt and clung stubbornly to the ground. Daylight was also gray and shrouded with clouds.

I liked working in the cafe well enough. My aunt, while not pampering me, treated me fairly and did not demand more of me than she did of the other two waitresses, Edith and Gisele. But the hours were long and hard. One of us rose each morning early, to go down and build up the fires in the big kitchen. The range there would act as a furnace for the whole cafe, nearly incinerating the poor cook, Monsieur Raspail,whose quick temper rose with the heat, and my aunt, who feverishly presided over pots and pans, preparing soups and cassoulets and roasts for the day. The cafe was not a fine restaurant, rather a modest place where working men could be sure of getting a good meal for very little money. They were served generous portions, with plenty of crusty bread from the nearby baker around the corner.

For the most part the men who came for meals were decent. I quickly learned how to avoid the others who with sly winks and groping hands reached for me whenever I walked past. My aunt was an expert in letting them know straightaway that she tolerated no foolishness. The men realized the food was good and by and large, took no chances that would banish them from the cafe.

So far, so good, I thought of my new life, proud that I could send my francs home each week, delivered by the farmer with his wagon who came from Saint Remy to Arles for the market, bringing livestock and produce to sell. The other waitresses, Edith and Gisele, with whom I shared a room upstairs, were of a good sort. They were looking for husbands, and sometimes went out after closing with men who were cafe regulars. Edith was a great gossip. I realized she would probably be telling tales about me when she whispered to me of the deplorable state of Gisele's tattered undergarments. So I was wary.

Gisele seemed harmless enough though a little dim. She had trouble remembering who had ordered what at the tables and could not keep straight the number of glasses of *vin ordinaire* each diner took. Unfortunately her face blossomed with pimples and one eye looked off in another direction in a disconcerting way. But her heart was kind.

I was helping her clear the last dishes from her table. It was almost closing time and my aunt and Edith had already gone upstairs. It was Edith's turn to build up the fires the next morning. It had started snowing again and most of the men had left for home. Suddenly the door of the cafe swung open and two men staggered in, their caps and faces dusted with snow and pinched with cold. In the flurry of frigid air which blew in, the men lurched and stumbled, their eyes unaccustomed to the light. Suddenly the taller of the two men fell forward and crumpled to the floor.

"Quick! Wine! I found him almost frozen outside the train station," his companion cried, a man I recognized as a regular diner. "He's either freezing to death or starving. Maybe both!"

And that is when I first saw the painter, Vincent Van Gogh.

CHAPTER TWO

I stood above the man, looking down at him. He reminded me of a large, golden bear. His face and neck were burnished from long hours in the sun. His hair and eyebrows were yellow like the sun, even the bristles covering the lower part of his face were yellow, for he had not shaved for several days. I noticed the hairs on his hands were golden also. In Provence, a land settled many centuries ago by Greeks, such light colored hair and eyes seemed strange to me. Where could the stranger be from? I wondered as I touched my own dark hair and my cheek, as brown as an almond.

As the men raised up his head and poured wine between his lips his eyelids fluttered open. Startled, I looked into the bluest, most piercing eyes I had ever seen. They focused and seemed to burn right through me. Blushing, I quickly stepped back. Gisele hurried to his side, murmuring softly and helping to raise him to his feet and guide him to a chair at one of the tables near the door. By this time, everyone in the cafe was crowding around.

"Stand back! Give him room!" Gisele cried in a proprietary way, emboldened perhaps because my aunt and Edith were not on the scene. "I will bring him a plate of stew," she announced.

Somewhat revived by the wine, the man began spooning the stew to his mouth, slowly at first, then ravenously. It became apparent that he was near starving. After finishing, he wiped his lips with a napkin and leaned back, replete.

"My good friends," he said, "You have saved me. I had been wandering about all day looking for a room without success. Then I came upon a mother and child in the cold, begging. I gave them what money I had, then made my way to the train station, thinking to spend the night in the warmth of the station. But it was locked for the night, with my belongings inside. I was left alone on the streets of Arles when this good man found me." He nodded toward the man who had brought him in.

"What are you doing in Arles?" one of the men asked him.

"I came to Arles to find a place in the sun," he answered thoughtfully, then added, "Perhaps I was somewhat premature in that wish as it is snowing." Nobody laughed but me. "You see, I am an artist. I paint pictures."

He said it as though that would explain everything. I saw a few of the men squirm and look at each other warily. As if reading the skepticism in their faces he looked around the circle and said simply, "I am Vincent Van Gogh. I come from Holland. My brother Theo supports me. He is an art dealer in Paris. You need not fear that I will be a burden to you with my lack of funds. Theo will send me money as he always has." He was completely relaxed and confident as he spoke. There was a child-like innocence in his face and in his voice.

There was an uneasy shuffling of feet as the listeners digested this bit of information. In their world, men earned their bread by the sweat of their brow. They knew nothing of men who painted pictures. Embarrassed, they looked at each other and made signs as if to go. Even the good Samaritan who brought him to the cafe suddenly mumbled good night and vanished through the door with the others. They did not want to be involved, I thought. Someone had to take charge.

"You can sleep here, on the floor in front of the stove in the kitchen. It will be warm there," I said quickly, finding my voice.

"Edith will come in to build up the fires about six in the morning. I know my aunt would not turn you away."

I spoke with a confidence I hardly felt. I had already witnessed Aunt Titi arguing heatedly to pare a few centimes off the butcher's bill, and the baker's too, come to that. She drove a hard bargain. But she also went to mass every Sunday. She could not turn out a homeless person on such a cold night. I knew she could not. At least, I hoped she could not! Such were my thoughts as Gisele and I saw the stranger bedded down, his jacket serving as a pillow, in front of the embers. Then we slowly made our way up the stairs to the little room under the eaves where Edith was snoring noisily.

*   *   *

I was awakened early the next morning by a loud scream from below. It was Edith of course, who had come upon the painter when she went down to build up the fires. Quickly I jumped up, throwing my shawl around my shoulders, and hurried downstairs, hoping to quiet her with an explanation before Aunt Titi came running. All could have been avoided if only I had awakened when she got out of bed to dress and go downstairs. Silently I bemoaned my sound sleeping habits as I managed to calm Edith and reassure the painter, who had received a nasty shock when Edith let out a scream.

Soon the three of us were drinking steaming cups of coffee and eating slices of bread which I toasted over the open fire. Van Gogh had the manners of a courtier I thought, treating us like royalty and not as two poor serving girls in a small cafe near the railroad station. He wanted to know our names and where we came from, what our ages were and how we happened to be working at the cafe. In five minutes I learned more about Edith than I had known in the week I had been in Arles. And all the while the alert blue eyes scrutinized everything. He studied our faces as though memorizing every feature, filing away the color of our hair, our skin, our eyes, the shape of a neck, how the hair fell from the crowns of our heads.

I had never encountered such a person before. His clothes were worn and paint-spattered, the clothes of a workman, although they were clean, albeit somewhat rumpled. Poor Edith was tongue-tied. She was in awe of this man who looked so fierce and acted so gentle.

Van Gogh rose to leave, saying he must be on his way to reclaim his belongings and seek out a place to stay. But he said he would return to thank my aunt for her hospitality. He took his leave gracefully and we watched him go, hardly knowing what to make of him.

Later that day when I returned to the cafe from the baker's shop with the day's order of bread, he was sitting with Aunt Titi at the table with the cash box where she stationed herself in the afternoons and evenings after the meal preparations were complete. I need not have worried that Aunt Titi would be cross. Van Gogh won her over at once with his honest charm. It was as though some saint lived inside that big, yellow bear of a man, I thought. In the early days, I easily fell prey to Vincent's winning ways.

He told us he had sent a telegram to his brother Theo, telling him about giving away his money. He was confident Theo would send more in a day or two. Meanwhile, he wondered if Mme. Ginoux would be willing to accept a painting in exchange for meals, just until he could get on his feet?

I watched Aunt Titi's eyes narrow while she thought over the proposition. I knew well enough what was running through her practical mind. But what if his paintings turned out to be worthless? Even so, it was tempting to think of having the cafe painted with the tables filled and the girls bustling about, apron strings flying as they waited on the diners. That would surely make her place distinctive, to be painted by an artist straight from Paris!

"All right," she answered. "I'll feed you for one week—one week—if you will paint me a scene of the inside of the cafe, a good one, mind!"

"I can only paint what I see," Vincent said simply, turning up the palms of his hands, like giant paws. He seemed as guileless as a newborn baby.

I admitted to myself as I stacked the *baguettes* on the shelf that I was attracted to him, partly because he was so unlike any man I had ever seen before. His very appearance presented such a dichotomy. He was like a young Saint Bernard puppy, clumsy but anxious to please. There was a wistful, yearning quality about Vincent. I imagined his eyes told me he had never received love like the love that welled up inside him; he had never found someone to return his love. As you can see, I was ready for fantasy.

Such rubbish, you say. A sixteen year old, thinking such things! Shame! But I have promised myself to be as honest as I can in putting everything down. Even then, when I first met Van Gogh, I had the feeling that our lives would run close to each other, how close I was not sure.

*   *   *

Vincent worked on the painting of the cafe in the room he had managed to rent on Place Lamartine. He told us the room was small and cramped, but at least it was a roof over his head and he was grateful to have it.

As February melted into March, there were signs of spring in the Midi. One day Vincent came to the cafe bringing several large branches of peach blossoms which he presented to Aunt Titi with a flourish. She was pleased in spite of her pique at his slowness in finishing the cafe painting.

"Soon, Madame Ginoux," he always answered her inquiries. "A painting cannot be rushed, and I am much slower painting from my head. I am working on some complicated color theories for the painting also." So she had to be content.

Vincent was scrupulous in paying for his meals after that first week. My aunt could not resist pressing second helpings on him, presenting him with little delicacies that were her specialty, like a wedge of *brie*, a serving of her *pate*.

"His eyes look so hungry," she murmured, sailing by me with her offering. I said nothing but thought food was not exactly what Van Gogh was hungering for, if I were any judge.

The painting, presented at last, was not a success. He called it "The Night Cafe" and expounded on its somber meaning to my aunt. In his picture, the cafe was all but deserted. Gloomy red walls and light from an overhanging lamp put the faces into eerie relief. They looked like lonely cadavers, those faces. Van Gogh tried to explain.

"I admit that the picture is not pretty. In fact, it is one of the ugliest I have done but its principle is important. I have tried to express the terrible passions of humanity by means of color, red and green. The room is blood red with a green billiard table in the middle. There are the four lemon yellow lamps with a glow of orange and green. Everywhere there is clash and contrast of those alien reds and greens. The cook, Monsieur Raspail, is alone in a corner of the room. His white clothes turn lemon yellow or pale, luminous green in the light. The faces of the few customers are lemon yellow as well. It is a picture about alienation and loneliness."

Vincent looked longingly at my aunt but she was not impressed. She had expected a room full of happy diners at flower-bedecked tables rather than the terrible passions of humanity. It was a cruel disappointment, but to her credit she rallied and thanked him prettily for his efforts. She took the painting to her room where it lived for years behind the *armoire*.

But as I looked at Vincent's face during the little presentation scene, I saw bitter disappointment there also. Would the world never understand his message? That is what must have been running through his head. It was all I could do to keep from taking his hand and whispering to him that I understood.

That evening, as the cafe closing time approached, Edith asked permission to go for a stroll around the arena. The arena, built when the Romans occupied Arles, was a favorite place to walk and a meeting place for the young people of the town. She promised to be back soon after eleven and said she would lock up carefully.

"*Oh, Oui,*" said my aunt absent-mindedly as she tallied up the day's receipts. "Charles again?" Charles was the name of the house painter Edith favored who was a regular at the cafe. You could set a watch by his unvarying habits. He must have been years older than Edith. My aunt did not even notice when Edith failed to reply. But I did.

I followed Edith with my eyes as she hurried upstairs to get her shawl. When she came down, her limp brown hair was fluffed up and tied with a pink ribbon. She had pinched her cheeks so that they bloomed a becoming rose color. She actually looked pretty, if she could remember to keep her mouth closed, I thought spitefully, for her teeth were brown and broken. I certainly did not begrudge Edith a walk around the arena with Charles.

But I knew it was not Charles she was meeting. It was Vincent. I had seen him whisper to her earlier, seen her face light up. I was sure he had asked her to meet him.

CHAPTER THREE

I heard Edith at the outside door with him about midnight. There was a lot of giggling and Edith's frantic shushing to quiet him.

"Careful or you'll waken Madame Ginoux," she said.

"Do the old tyrant good," he answered, his speech slurred. "Teach her not to denigrate my work," he said in an aggrieved tone.

"Ah, she didn't mean any harm. She just didn't know what to make of it. She expected something different."

"I paint what I see," Vincent answered belligerently.

"Sure you do, anyway, give a girl another kiss, how about it?"

"I paint what I see!" he thundered. "Can't anyone in this whole world understand?" There was the sound of footsteps on the cobbles, then silence.

"Well I never!" Edith exclaimed. "The blighter's gone!"

Edith locked the door and quickly came upstairs, undressing in the dark and falling into her cot. The smell of wine filled the room. Soon she was snoring in harmony with Gisele and I was left awake to brood on my disappointment in Vincent. He did not sound quite so courtly a few minutes earlier at the door. And I could not help but feel sorry for Edith who must have had a disappointing evening with all that wine drinking and Vincent's foul temper. It was my turn to get up early and build up the fires. When I came back upstairs for a few minutes more sleep, I heard Edith and Gisele whispering. ". . . I think he has a screw loose. He blathered the whole time about the wretched picture when he wasn't swigging on the wine. We had a cuddle or two but I had the feeling his brain was a million miles away." She stopped abruptly when I entered the room. I pretended I'd heard nothing.

*   *   *

By late April Provence was coming alive with blossoming red poppies in the fields, white and pink clovers, yellow sun drops. I asked Aunt Titi if I could go home on the weekend to see my mother and brothers and sisters.

"We'll ask the farmer to give you a lift when he comes to market on the Saturday. He'll bring you back early Monday morning," she said. Silently I thanked the heavens for my kind aunt.

All that week I hummed under my breath as I flew between the kitchen and the tables in the cafe. I was going home! My thoughts were on the visit as I served Raoul, a rough wagon driver from Saintes-Maries-Sur-Mer who came to Arles regularly with a load of fish to sell at the market. Raoul had taken a liking to me, but I did not return this interest. I could not bear to be near him. His hands always smelled of fish and he was likely to be unshaven, his fleshy jowls covered in a dark, bristly shadow. With his stomach hanging over his belt and black hairy arms he reminded me of a fat spider.

Raoul prided himself on being a Romeo. I'd heard him boast to the men of his sexual conquests, rolling his dark eyes suggestively, running his hands through his wavy, greasy hair. He fancied himself irresistible to women. I set down a sizzling dish of *escargot* sputtering in garlic butter, my thoughts far away, and he seized the moment to put his hairy arm around my waist as he murmured, "Come, *ma petite.*"

Furious at myself for my inattention, I struggled to wrench free from his grip. He had timed his playful assault when Aunt Titi was in the kitchen, helping the cook get the evening roast into the ovens.

"Let me go!" I cried, louder than I had intended, causing several diners at nearby tables to look up in surprise. Like statues they sat, leering, but nobody came to my aid, except for Vincent. Sitting alone at a nearby table in the corner, he quickly arose and stood beside me.

"*Mademoiselle* would like to return to the kitchen now," he said quietly in a voice that was resonant with meaning. The blue eyes like blue fire bored into Raoul who jumped quickly to his feet, knocking over his chair. But before chaos could erupt, my aunt sailed in bearing a steaming cassoulet.

"Your lamb, Monsieur Raoul. Here it is straight from the oven, a dish fit for a king!" Raoul hesitated for a split second. Then, thinking better of it, he righted his chair and sat down abruptly and began to attack his food.

My knees felt like jelly as I hurried toward the kitchen, silently blessing Vincent for coming to my aid. The resentment I'd felt earlier toward him dissolved. Even if he had asked Edith instead of me to walk, he had stood up for me against the dragon Raoul. He was back up on a pedestal again in my mind.

*   *   *

Word came from my mother by way of the farmer from Saint Remy that Francine was sick with a fever and that I should postpone my visit for a few weeks until she was recovered. I had looked forward to seeing my family so much! Worry about Francine's frail health enveloped me. Francine, with the small, heart-shaped face, swinging black braids, her tender smile. I missed her more than any of the others and feared for her health.

"Do not worry, Minette," said Aunt Titi patting my arm. "She will be well in no time! You can take a walk to the countryside on Sunday. It will be lovely now." It was true. The wildflowers were blooming, the leaves were at their freshest, decked out in shiny green which had not yet been coated with dust, birds filled the air with their songs.

But how could I enjoy my time alone? Even Edith or Gisele would be company, but they had made plans of their own. I would have to go alone. I trudged up to my room to bed that night feeling homesick, still undecided as to where I should go. Should I visit the Alyscamps, the old Roman burying ground with its huge trees and melancholy paths lined with empty, ancient sarcophagi? Or I could visit the ancient church of Saint Trophime, whose stone column headings of the cloister were prized as perfect examples of Gothic art.

During the night it came to me in a dream what I should do on my free day. A few kilometers away from Arles was the ruined abbey of Montmajour. I had heard Van Gogh talk of the beauty of the ruins, the surrounding fields. I would go to Montmajour abbey and see for myself!

The air was fresh and warm as I left Arles on the market road toward the abbey. I carried a package of bread and cheese and wore an old straw hat my aunt loaned to me.

"Don't feel you have to hurry back!" she called. "Enjoy your day."

My spirits were high as I walked along in the sunshine, but I remembered to say a special prayer for Francine. The bonds between us were very strong. I thought of her frequent sick spells. I could not shrug it off as my mother did, saying it was the will of God. Somehow I felt that if Francine had more warm clothing and nourishing food—milk and butter and cheese everyday—she would be better able to ward off sick spells.

From some distance I could see the ruined abbey of Montmajour high on the plain as I approached, with plantations of pine and olive below it. As I drew nearer I could see empty arched windows, roofless rooms alive with blooming flowers, fig trees nudging the walls, trees on which hundreds of tiny fruits were growing.

Up close, the ruins were even more beautiful, half covered in twisting vines with red wildflowers springing up everywhere. I clambered happily in and out of the cubicles which were open to the sun, climbed crumbling stairways leading nowhere. They gave me splendid views of the surrounding fields. Far below, I could make out tiny sprouts of green beginning to emerge in the straight rows. Drifts of sweet clover and yellow sundrops framed the ribbon of the road like lacy ruffles. How could anyone not wish to be a painter here, I thought, thinking of Vincent and wondering if he too was out working in this glorious living panorama of renewal spread before my eyes.

I looked up and saw that the sun was high in the sky. It must be nearing midday. I thought of my bread and cheese and suddenly craved a cool drink from the spring. I was grateful for Aunt Titi's wide-brimmed straw hat for the sun was beating down with a vengeance. I quickly made my way to the clumps of willows growing in thickets beside the banks of the little stream.

I sat down beside the gurgling little stream as it sang a music all of its own and ate my bread and cheese, drinking from the cool, clear water. Strangely I did not feel lonely or afraid. It was as though the spot I had chosen was a holy one, close to the abbey ruins so as to be protected. I felt a calm, a peace I had not experienced since my father's death. I could think about Saint Remy and all the happy memories—the love of my parents, the joys of being together even though life was hard and filled with backbreaking work. I remembered a day like today, a Sunday, when we all had taken a picnic to a small lake and had sat warming ourselves in the sun after wading in the chilly waters. Being away from the bustle of the cafe cleared my thoughts and I gave thanks for the many good memories in my life.

I leaned on my arm, stretched out beside the stream and must have fallen asleep for I awoke much later with the sun low in the sky and a decided chill hovering in the air. I sat up and looked about. Perched on a boulder, not ten feet away from me, sat Vincent, quietly sketching in a notebook.

He continued to sketch in a leisurely way looking at the stream, speaking in a calm voice.

"You know, Minette, you really should not come into this secluded area alone. All kinds of lawless people use the willows to hide in. It could be dangerous." I should have been grateful for his concern, but I reacted like a spoiled child criticized by a parent.

"I am old enough to take care of myself," I blurted out, nettled by his words. "Besides, we are near a holy place. The ruins of the abbey are just there." Vincent let out a loud guffaw which upset me even more.

"So you think the ghosts of the holy sisters and brothers will protect you?" His eyes crinkled up at the corners and he laughed again. "Minette, you are a child!"

"It would be blasphemy to doubt God's protection!" I cried out angrily. "What are you, an infidel?" I was so angry I was careless with my words. I cared nothing for what I said.

In an instant his face crumpled and the line of his jaw hardened. "I am no infidel," he said, in a low, guttural tone. "There was a time when I almost became a priest." He spoke so softly I had trouble hearing him. Had I heard rightly? My mouth fell open.

"A priest! Whatever do you mean?" I looked at him in surprise.

"Well, not exactly a priest, but a preacher. It was in the Borinage, the coal mining district of Belgium. It was years ago."

"Why did you give it up?" I asked. Vincent looked me straight in the eye.

"Because I failed. Failed my examinations, failed my trial period, failed God, you could say." His eyes took on a faraway look. "I believe in God, but not the god of that bigoted, self-righteous bunch at the church in Belgium. I tried to help those poor, starving people in the coal fields, I really did. But it was not their way, so they got rid of me."

I sat looking at Vincent, thinking how much this man had

been beaten down in spite of all his good intentions. It did not seem fair.

"And that is when you turned to painting?" I asked.

"Yes. I worship with my brush now. The outdoors becomes my church." I stood up and walked over to where he sat sketching. "I do not think you are a failure, Vincent. Not at all." Vincent quickly stood up and put his arms around me. We stood there not speaking and the only sounds were bird calls and the soft whispering of the willows ruffled by gentle winds. My heart was beating a tattoo and I feared Vincent would hear it, but he said nothing and then took a step back, as though pulling away from his feelings.

"What is it?" I cried, feeling hurt.

"Nothing, Minette," he answered. "Nothing at all. Remember, I am your friend. What I have told you I've never told anyone else, not even my family." I could tell, he was trying to scale back our feelings.

"Not even Theo?" I was curious in spite of myself.

"Theo knows, but we don't talk about it. It was so painful I want to keep it buried, hidden. It still wounds me deeply when I think about it."

"But they were wrong!" I said. "You are kindness itself. What could they have been thinking of?"

"Ah, Minette, you are a child. So pure. You do not know the ways of the world. Dark currents course inside me, I know it. I am not worthy even to be called your friend." The look of sadness I showed must have moved him, for he quickly took my hands saying, "Come now, we must be happy and make your day one to remember with joy. Let's tell each other stories as we walk back to Arles." He turned and began packing up his notebook and pencils in his rucksack.

As we walked toward Arles in the late afternoon's fading light he told me more about himself. About his beloved brother Theo who worked for the gallery firm of Goupil in Paris, about his mother and his father, a pastor, who had died two years earlier. He talked of his life in Holland, the look of the landscape there, the sea and its closeness to all parts of Dutch life. He talked of the frantic life of Paris, living with his brother, and how the fast pace of the city upset him and grated on his nerves.

"As for Arles," he said thoughtfully, I have terrible lucidity here at moments when nature is so glorious. Times like that, I am hardly conscious of myself. My pictures come to me like in a dream. Life is enchanting!" His eyes told me he was transported far away at that moment.

"And are you not lonely, living by yourself, not having many friends, other men I mean?" I hoped somehow to bring his thoughts around to me.

"Yes, Minette, of course I feel the loneliness. I feel that even sometimes when I am surrounded by people. But I have my dreams."

"And what are those dreams, Vincent?"

"Listen," he said, taking my hand, his blue eyes shining. "I have told no one this, not even Theo yet. But I have found a little house on Place Lamartine near my rooms, where I can set up a *maison d'artiste*, a house for artists where I can live and paint in the company of my artist friends from Paris." His eyes were gleaming with a light that was almost fanatical. A shiver of alarm went through me, disappointment as well, for Vincent's thoughts were not of me at all!

"How can you afford the rent of such a house," I questioned, my aunt's practicality asserting itself suddenly.

Vincent smiled and said confidently, "Theo will help me."

The distance back to Arles seemed very short, we had so much to talk about. There were a number of wagons on the road. As one of the wagons rumbled past a loud voice called out, "So this is where you sneak off, when you leave the cafe!"

The man turned back to leer at us as we stopped in the road, startled at his words. Raoul! And with his insinuating words he had made our being together something furtive, tawdry, something cheap. I hated Raoul at that moment for spoiling the lovely mood of the day.

Vincent shrugged, muttering, "He is a bad sort, that fellow."

*   *   *

Several days after my excursion to Montmajour abbey my aunt
called me to her room one evening shortly after the cafe closed. As
I entered she asked me if I had a good time on my trip.

"Oh, yes, Aunt," I answered. "The ruins are beautiful. There
is so much to see!

"From the top of the ruins the view over the plain, the
Camargue, is breath-taking." We had spoken of this earlier. What
else, I wondered, could she possibly want to know?

"Raoul told Edith that he saw you and Monsieur Van Gogh
walking together along the road to Arles." She paused. Suddenly I
was seething inside. Edith! The Snake! Typical of her to go tattling
to Aunt Titi instead of asking me about it!

"Yes, Aunt," I answered calmly. "It is true. We ran into each
other by chance as I was preparing to return to Arles. He had been
sketching in the area. We walked back together."

"Minette, I know you will think me a meddling old lady for
what I am about to say, but I am going to say it all the same. You
like Monsieur Van Gogh, I can tell, but you should go very slowly,
my dear. He is not what he seems to be." My cheeks flamed up. I
could feel them. How dare she tell me what I should and should
not do! She was not my parent.

As though reading my thoughts, she said softly, "I know I am
not your mother, but you are with me here, and I must keep your
best interests foremost. Last night, Minette, your friend Van Gogh
became drunk at the town *Maison de Tolerance* and had to be
removed by the police for fighting. He was taken home from the
brothel and warned not to let it happen again. Had this not
happened, I would have ignored Edith's tattle tale."

My face fell at her words. My throat choked up and I could
hardly breathe. She clucked sympathetically.

"I know, I know, *ma petite,* it is hard to bear. Monsieur Van

Gogh is not a well person. He suffers from a strange malady. It is as though he is two different people, they say. One minute docile and kind, the next minute like a raging lion. The Prefect told me this when he called, not an hour ago."

I managed to listen to my aunt without screaming and to get through the evening somehow by keeping my face a mask. Only when I lay in the narrow cot in the darkness listening to the snores of Edith and Gisele did I give way to my feelings. Tears rolled silently down my cheeks.

What horrible things they were saying about Vincent. Could it be true that he visited brothels? I recalled what he had said to me as we sat under the willows beside the stream. Something about dark currents coursing within him. Is this what he meant? I remembered his drunkenness the night he took Edith out. And why did I care so much? Silent tears wet my pillow and it was nearly dawn when at last I fell into a restless sleep.

CHAPTER FOUR

From that time onward, I was careful to keep my feelings about Vincent locked inside. My aunt was a lovable woman, but she was also a controlling person, and I knew better than to displease her. My mother depended desperately on the few francs I earned, and I could not fail her. She sent word to us that by another miracle Francine had been restored to them and my visit was planned for later in May.

When Vincent came to the cafe, almost every day, I was pleasant but impersonal. I tried to keep from looking at him except in the most offhand way. No one, not even Edith the Snake, could find anything to gossip about now, I thought smugly. But they could not control my thoughts.

One day Vincent arrived unexpectedly carrying his painting paraphernalia. He came at the slow time when the midday diners had left and the preparations for the evening had not begun.

"Madame Ginoux," he said, bowing, "I have come to paint your portrait."

"Here? Now?" gushed Aunt Titi, obviously pleased. Her fingers touched her hair. "A pleasure, Monsieur Van Gogh! I am honored. Give me five minutes." She vanished upstairs. Vincent, I realized, was trying to make amends for the Night Cafe picture.

Quickly Vincent set up his easel and readied the canvas. Whipping out his palette, he expertly squeezed out green, chrome yellow, black, white and several reds on to it. He poured linseed oil into a small tin attached to the palette.

"You are going to paint the portrait right on the spot?" I asked, wondering if he would be able to work quickly. Aunt Titi had the evening dinner to supervise.

"Right, Minette. I told Madame Ginoux that I worked better in front of the motif rather than from memory. I am prepared to show her the truth of that statement." He seemed so calm, so confident, I marveled at his poise.

With a rustling of her skirts, Aunt Titi reappeared. She had changed into her best black bombazine and had pinned a snowy, freshly laundered fichu at her bosom. Her hair pulled severely back from her face, was caught in back by the small headdress of laces and ribbons worn by *Les Arlesiennes*. She looked magnificent. Her large, luminous eyes, her beautiful *cafe au lait* skin set her figure off to perfection. Quickly Vincent seated her at her table and placed two books from his rucksack in front of her, "so you will be able to occupy your hands while I work," he explained.

At once he began broadly sketching in the figure with great slashes of his brush. The intensity he displayed almost frightened me. The steel of the blue eyes glinted as he worked. The eyes left her face only to look quickly at the canvas. It was apparent nothing else existed in this charged, private world of Vincent working.

Edith and Gisele had already disappeared upstairs to rest by the time he arrived, but I had no intention of joining them. I wanted to watch Vincent at work. I found myself mesmerized by the frenzy of his assault on the canvas. He worked at fever pitch, first slashing on brushload after brushload of chrome yellow for the background. The figure itself would be a *tour de force* in black. My aunt's jet black hair and dress made a marvelous foil for her coffee and cream skin color, which Vincent lightened just a little on his canvas.

The colors of the flesh tones were amazing to me. Green,

alizarin, ultramarine, cobalt—all went into the creamy mixture and as a result her skin took on the depth and texture of living flesh.

Vincent did not notice anything or anyone as he worked. Once he commanded Aunt Titi, "Put your left hand on your cheek, the elbow on the table," and she quickly complied. Of course he spent more time on the face, taking up smaller and smaller brushes, delicately stroking the canvas. A final assault enriching the gold and yellow of the background and the painting was finished. In an amazing three-quarters of an hour! He threw down his brushes and stepped back.

"It will be called "The Arlesienne," he said softly. My aunt hurried over to look. We were dumbfounded by the raw power of the work, the bravura strokes of his brush and the tender, yearning quality he had given my aunt's face. Maybe we did not understand Vincent's painting, but we recognized his genius. He had captured the essence of my aunt. It was an astounding likeness. Graciously she thanked him, inviting him on the spot to a celebration dinner the following evening. She treasured this masterpiece the rest of her life.

*   *   *

The dinner was a grand affair. Aunt Titi invited the postman Roulin and his wife who had become friends of Vincent, the Cure, and her two nephews, children of her sister who lived in Avignon. I was put in charge of the table. I went to the fields to pick wildflowers for the centerpiece, arranged the best plates and linens, placed snowy napkins at each place. The finished table was lovely, the blue and yellow of the flowers outlined by the white cloths.

Vincent appeared in a freshly laundered shirt for the evening, although there were old paint stains on it. The young nephews, darkly handsome, seemed like genial twins, a bit juvenile perhaps, but my aunt praised them to the skies in front of me, as though she thought I might take note, for each one represented "a good catch" she told me seriously in private. They would be storekeepers like their father in Avignon, if all went according to plan. They were learning the business of a cloth merchant in Arles, a friend of their father. My aunt's portrait stood in pride of place on an easel at one end of the room, drying. It was duly praised and admired by all the guests. Gisele and Edith were to be waitresses at the table, while I handled the other tables and Monsieur Raspail held out alone in the kitchen.

The diners were treated to a clear fish soup, followed by a superb saddle of veal with roasted potatoes crusty on the outside, soft within, the tiniest of green beans not more than a few inches long, and tiny carrots. Salad and cheese courses followed with a final dessert course, *Coupe Helene,* a triumph of poached pears and whipped cream over a custard, then coffee in the minuscule cups.

As the evening drew to a close, the nephews whispered to Aunt Titi and she beckoned to me. "Edmond and Hubert wish to go to the arena. Will you go for a breath of fresh air with them?"

I nodded and went for my shawl. The others left the cafe with us, Vincent and the Cure walking with the Roulins. Unexpectedly Vincent joined us, asking if he might go along. At the arena, we met other young people, new friends of Edmond and Hubert. Soon we were strolling in a large party and Vincent maneuvered to be at my side. In great excitement he told me he had persuaded his brother Theo to rent the small house on Place Lamartine. He would be moving his studio at once, and would begin living there as soon as he was able to get a bed, a chair, and a few other housekeeping essentials.

"It is the first time in all of my life, Minette, that I have had a home of my own!" He was exultant. "Now I can truly welcome artists to a School of the South! Don't you see, Minette, we artists will work together, help each other, and we shall be better artists for it."

Privately I wondered if his brother would be willing to pay the expenses of such a colony, but I could not say anything. How could I interject even one tiny doubt or question that might dash his happy, child-like hopes. There was a trusting quality, an innocence about Vincent that I found so compelling. It was part of his charm, I thought.

Somehow in walking we became separated from the others. I reminded Vincent I should be returning to the cafe.

"Ah, Minette, you are so good to listen to my ramblings. And now I have lost Madame's nephews for you! She will not be pleased." I reassured him that it did not matter and he took my arm and guided me quickly to the cafe.

"Will you come for a look at my little house when I have it arranged?" he asked. I answered that I would gladly come, wondering at the same time how I could manage it. Perhaps during the slow time in the afternoon, if I could get away.

"Bless you, Minette," Vincent said as we came to the door of the cafe. "It is so good to talk with you since my confidant, my brother, is so far away. You understand better than anyone how I feel! We are soulmates!" He embraced me quickly and planted a kiss on my forehead. Then he left.

I took his words and hugged them to my heart. They were not love words, but they were all I had, and that quick kiss was precious to me.

*   *   *

Vincent was spending a week at the fishing village of Saintes-Maries-sur-Mer on the Mediterranean, a trip he had dreamed of for some time. He wrote me several letters describing the village so beautifully that I could see it plainly in my mind.

"I am writing to you from Saintes-Maries-sur-Mer. I am on the shore of the Mediterranean Sea at last. The sea has the coloring of a mackerel, changeable I mean. You don't always know if it is green or violet, you can't even say it's blue, because the next moment the changing reflection has taken on a tinge of blue or gray. I have board and lodging for four francs a day (that certainly will please

Theo!). The shore here is sandy, no cliffs nor rocks—like Holland, but without the dunes, and bluer.

"I do not think there are one hundred houses in the village, or town. The chief building, after the old church and an ancient fortress, is the barracks. Many of the houses have quaint roofs of thatch."

How precious his letters were to me. I kept them hidden in my pocket and read them over and over whenever I could, in secret. It goes without saying I had never known anyone remotely like Van Gogh. I wanted to learn from him all I could about painting, about the books he read and talked of, about life! He seemed more alive than any person I had ever met in all of my life. He closed one of the letters this way:

"One night I went for a walk by the sea along the empty shore. I wish you had been there with me. It was beautiful. The deep blue sky was flecked with clouds of a blue deeper than the fundamental blue of intense cobalt, and others of a clearer blue like the blue whiteness of the Milky Way. In the blue depth the stars were sparkling greenish yellow, white, rose, brighter and flashing more like jewels than they seem to be in Arles: opals, you might call them, emeralds, lapis, rubies, sapphires." What I would not give to see the world as Vincent saw it!

When Vincent returned to Arles he brought a half dozen finished paintings of boats along the shore, the quaint houses with roofs of thatch, the church. And he left another four drying at his lodgings. They were too wet to be moved. He planned to collect them when he passed through on an excursion to Tarascon he hoped to make.

*   *   *

As the weekend of my visit home arrived, I thought of how my life had changed as I jolted along in the farmer's wagon on the way to Saint Remy. Leaves on the plane trees lining the main street of the town danced in the sunlight and I could see at the end of the street the little cottage which had been my home all of my life.

During the entire visit I felt like something of a stranger, though I had been away only a few months. It frightened me a little that I had so quickly grown accustomed to my life in Arles, so much so that my brothers and sisters, except for Francine, seemed like strangers. I still felt close to my mother of course.

Francine kept by my side and when I was seated, she would sit on the floor in front of me and place her head in my lap. I was dismayed at how pale and sad her face was. I longed to see more color in her cheeks. If anything, she seemed more frail, more ephemeral. She had survived the sick spell earlier, but I worried about the delicacy of her health.

On this visit, I slept in the old bed downstairs with my mother and we were able to whisper our concerns to each other after the others had gone to sleep.

"How are you managing, *Maman*?" I asked, for I could see that food was very scarce. Earlier that evening, the eyes of my brothers and sisters widened with hunger as I unpacked gifts from Aunt Titi: a cheese, a dozen eggs, a leaf-wrapped mound of butter, a small sack of sugar. How pleased they all looked as I sliced the bread, slathered it with butter, and sprinkled sugar on top.

"It is very hard, Minette," my mother answered. "The children do their best, but there is simply not enough to go around after the rent is paid. I have great hopes for the grain harvest this season. It should make things a bit easier, and get us through the winter."

I insisted on doing all of the ironing while I was there. It seemed the least I could do, everyone was so burdened with work. I gave the house a good scrubbing while Francine and I played word games together. Colette considered herself too grown up to join in. The last night, lying beside my mother, I caught myself actually anticipating my return to Arles. It came as a guilty shock for me to realize that the cafe, Arles, and yes, Vincent had become my world in my heart of hearts. Ashamed, I let the tears course down my cheeks and silently vowed to do more to help the brave, desperate woman at my side.

When I returned to Arles on the Monday morning I went

straight to Aunt Titi's room and asked her to let me take on the cafe laundry on my free afternoons. Silently she regarded me for a time, her lovely eyes seeking mine.

"You found them in need, then?" she said matter-of-factly.

"Yes."

"And what if you exhaust yourself working like a slave and get sick, and cannot do your job in the cafe?"

"I won't exhaust myself," I replied confidently. "I am young and strong and as healthy as an ox." My aunt stood, her long-fingered hands folded over the back of her chair.

"Then I will let you do the laundry two afternoons a week, during the slow time. But on Wednesday afternoons, I insist that you enjoy yourself. Get out, take walks, get away from work and the cafe. I will not have it said that Madame Ginoux is making a slave of her niece!"

I ran to her and put my arms around her. "Thank you, Aunt Titi, you are so good to me!"

"Nonsense. We are making a bargain. That's all, child. I'll pay you what I pay the laundress who does the work. And if the job is too much for you, we'll have to cancel the arrangement."

Fair enough, I thought. More francs to send home. I was elated.

CHAPTER FIVE

Aunt Titi was as good as her word. I went to the city wash house on the Tuesday and then ironed the linens on the Thursday afternoons in a corner of the big kitchen. Wednesday afternoons were free. If the weather was fine I could stroll in the town, or in the Alyscamps if the sun was beating down, for it was always shady and cool there. Aunt seemed more relaxed now about my friendship with Vincent. After he painted the marvelous portrait of her, her views softened a bit. Then, as far as she was able to determine, there had been no more incidents of fighting reported. She must have decided that whatever her doubts about Vincent had been, they were no longer valid. His behavior was impeccable.

How could she know that I still hung on his words, cherished the few letters he had written me, reading them until they fell apart. And I was longing for the time when I would visit his house. I would be ready, on my free Wednesday afternoon.

Edith and Gisele had placed me in a niche labeled "Madame's Favorite", and thought that as her niece I received special treatment, when they learned about the laundry and my free Wednesday afternoons. Actually they had far more leisure time than I. Edith was coming close to her dream of marriage, for she was going out regularly with Charles, the house painter.

She bragged to us constantly that once she was married, there would be no more waiting on tables, oh no. She would be keeping a shining house for her husband. Perhaps, she said slyly, she would invite us to come for coffee one day. These excursions of Edith into the future were laid out to us when we were in our cots in the darkened room, a captive audience, and could not escape her.

By taking on the cafe laundry I had made more work for myself, but the touching letter from my mother after I had sent the extra francs the first week made it seem worthwhile. So on Tuesday afternoons I loaded up table cloths and napkins into two large baskets and set out for the municipal wash house. It was a simple shed built right over the little stream from the river Rhone which ran through Arles, and the women knelt on hard stones, bending over the water, dipping their laundry in the cool, swiftly moving waters and beating it on the rocks lining the stream.

There was a lot of gossip and laughter. It was a sociable time for the women whose lives were so filled with the work of taking care of their children and keeping house they had no time to pay calls on each other. I kept a little aloof as they were older than I and acted superior because they were married.

Two women I had never seen before were washing opposite when I suddenly heard words that were of the greatest interest to me. They both lived on Place Lamartine and had been observing the strange Dutchman who was a painter of pictures, a man who seemed as docile as a dove, they said, but could quickly become volatile and rave like a caged lion.

"He works fixing up that house until all hours of the night," the one called Mauricette said. "Last night he was painting the walls. We could see through the window, plain as anything; he had candles set on the floor burning all around him. It's a wonder he doesn't burn the place down, working like that!"

"I wonder why he doesn't do the work in the daytime, when he can see better?" the other one asked.

"Oh, don't you know? He has to be painting his pictures in daylight. I've seen him working like a driven spirit, his eyes boring into the distance while he paints away at the Alpilles mountains beyond Arles. My Henri says he probably will try to paint the *mistral* next." Both of them laughed heartily at this.

But I knew to Vincent the wild, blowing winds of the *mistral* were no laughing matter, as I'd heard him lament their ferocity many times. And the wind was especially bad this year. So bad that it was impossible to set up an easel or pour out paint when it was blowing.

Suddenly the one called Mauricette bent close to her friend and said, "They say he takes women there, to that house of his."

"Oh, surely not!" the other answered, shocked.

"Oh, yes. You remember a while back he was in a fight at the brothel with some other men? The Prefect told him then to watch his step. They say now he invites his lady friends, so called, to visit him at the little house, instead of going to the brothel."

Seething inwardly at the scurrilous gossip, I was beating the same cloth viciously on the rocks until I realized what I was doing, seeing the amazed faces of the two women looking at me. I glowered at them but said nothing. It was so unfair to Vincent! Just because he was different from them. To spread such unsavory rumors about, rumors I was certain were untrue, made me feel resentful.

"Well," the timid one ventured, "It might be just gossip. He was kind to help me when Alphonse ran into the street and I had the baby in my arms. Quick as anything he went after Alphonse and brought him back, sitting on his shoulder. Alphonse loved it!"

Then Mauricette said she'd heard he had two personalities, good and bad. The trouble was, how could you be sure which one he was wearing? More laughter as I gritted my teeth and kept washing. Thankfully they finished soon and left.

After hearing all that the two women said, I decided not to keep waiting for a special invitation from Vincent to see the Little Yellow House. I would go the following afternoon and see for myself.

Maybe it will rain tomorrow (not likely) I thought. Maybe Aunt Titi will need me at the cafe (possible but not probable). Maybe the *mistral* will be blowing so hard I cannot venture out. I invented all sorts of reasons that would keep me away, for I felt a little *frisson* of fear when I thought of paying an unexpected call on Vincent. Anything could happen! But I knew in the end, I would go.

I did not dare change into different clothes that afternoon as I made ready to leave. That would have aroused suspicions all around. Instead, I simply waited for the time when the cafe was empty and walked nonchalantly out the door, strolling aimlessly along the road for a bit then making for Two, Place Lamartine.

I had thought about possibly encountering Mauricette or her friend. But Place Lamartine was deserted, its entire population either dining late or already into the siesta. Boldly I approached. As I had expected, it was a very small house, two windows showing in the upper floor, a window and a door below. The house was painted a sunny yellow, with shutters of the darkest viridian. The facade, though humble, had a certain presence which I liked very much.

I knocked firmly on the door and heard movement from the depths of the house. He was there! In a matter of seconds a paint-smeared Vincent stood before me, a large brush in his hand.

"Minette! What a surprise! Come in, you are welcome. I was planning to invite you and Madame Ginoux to see the house when it was more finished, but this is splendid! Come in!" Decisively I stepped inside, brushing away the thought which had been in the back of my mind ever since I determined to go, that an unmarried woman did not pay a call on a single man, or any man in fact, who lived alone.

He took me over every inch of the property, pride in his voice for something he was creating, as though the newly cleaned and whitewashed rooms were a painting he had labored over. The tiny sitting room downstairs would become the studio, he said. It had two chairs, a yellow ladderback and a brown painted chair with arms. The other room was the kitchen, bare except for an old stone sink, a scrubbed table and a small cupboard on the wall. The remains of a loaf of bread and a wedge of cheese lay on rough paper on the table. There was a small carafe of wine also. He had made a simple meal.

"There will be chairs here of course later," he said, "when funds are available. Theo has promised to send money soon. The second hand furniture dealer has some nice things." The walls were bare but freshly whitewashed. Vincent looked as proud as any housewife showing off her home.

"Come," he said. "Let me show you the upstairs." We climbed the steep stairs to an open area that was like a loft. Then there were two tiny rooms, large enough for cots or single beds, wash stands and a chair. One of the rooms had no furniture.

"Here is my bedroom," Vincent said proudly as he threw open the door of the larger room. The walls were painted a pale blue. The floor was covered in old, faded red tiles, shining clean. The bed and chair, another ladderback, were painted yellow and in the shuttered light, the sheets and pillowcases took on a greenish hue. A few clothes hung on pegs and a small mirror hung above the wash stand.

The beauty of that little room with the wonderful light, its simplicity, took my breath away. The light pronounced a benediction on all Vincent's efforts. It was a special place, a haven.

"Vincent," I said, searching for the right words, "You have made it such a happy place!" I could tell by the look in his eyes he was pleased by my words. Why, oh why cannot things go right for this man, I asked silently of whatever power ruled unseen over our lives. How can one who has so much to give be so misunderstood? I was quite cast down by the futility, the unfairness of it all. At the same time I marveled at his generous spirit, his kindness, his civility in spite of all the hardships he had to endure.

"Vincent," I said suddenly, walking closer to him, "can you help me? I am just a poor peasant girl, but I want to become something better. Can you teach me how to become a wiser person, tell me what books I should read. Could you talk to me about paintings? I want to be able to see nature the way you see it." I raised my eyes to his face.

"Minette, Minette," he said softly, taking my hands in his. "Do not speak so of yourself! I will not allow it! You are strong and brave and yes, wise. Your aunt has told me what you are doing to help your family. You have a sweet, unspoiled nature, untainted by the world. I would not have you change that. But if you like, I will try to tell you about books I have read and you may come with me when I paint and I will show you what I have learned."

He paused and smiled. "We will be comrades! Would you like that?"

His words were not the love words I was hoping for. I had imagined something in a more romantic vein, standing close together as we did in the little bedroom. I had hoped for a loving encounter . . . . But it was a beginning. Vincent surely had realized it was not the proper time or the place for any intimacy between us. To avoid any hint of embarrassment he gently turned away and walked toward the stairs.

"You will come back another time, Minette? And bring Madame Ginoux?" he quickly asked, descending the steep stairs.

"Yes, Vincent," I answered somewhat humbled, for I had discovered something about myself in that beautiful little upstairs bedroom. Vincent was a better person than I! Not his wish to take advantage of youth and inexperience when the opportunity presented itself. As I turned to leave he kissed my forehead. "Thank you, Minette, for believing in me."

I made my way to the cafe and pondered the little scene that had just played itself out on Place Lamartine. However the rest of the world might view Vincent, I had yet to see this gentle spirit as anything but upright and honorable, except perhaps for the interlude with Edith outside the door of the cafe. And on that occasion he had reason to be upset! His painting, the Night Cafe, had been unappreciated by his friend, my Aunt Titi.

I still believed Vincent cared for me but held back. Or was it nothing more than the care of a friend for another? Or the care of a brother for a sister? Just which was not so clear to me.

CHAPTER SIX

Vincent planned to work in the public gardens across from Place Lamartine the following week, he told me, having finished most of the decorating of the Little Yellow House. He planned to work until midday at his house, then go the short distance to the gardens in the afternoon, staying until sundown. He invited me to come and watch him paint on Wednesday afternoon and offered to tell me about the book he had just finished reading, a collection of essays on French painting by the de Goncourt brothers.

When I arrived at the gardens it was a few minutes before I spotted him, working in the shade of a big cypress tree. He was painting a pathway, a wide gravel walk edged by ancient cypresses and pines, interspersed with tree-like shrubs of oleander. He was wearing a straw hat with a wide brim, such as peasants wear, but he wore it with such panache! It suits him, I thought, as I approached.

As promised, he had brought the book on French paintings, and suggested I read to him the captions under the pictures and we could discuss them. After each paragraph, Vincent added his own thoughts about the painter and his work. In a short while my head was spinning; how could I remember all the details about so many painters? Vincent was quick to see my confusion.

"Do not fret, Minette, you will sort them out in time. The important thing is to look—really look—at the work. Try to discover what the artist wanted to express when he painted it. Was it love, joy, sadness, pain, anger? Always look for the emotion in a painting. I know the more I work on pastoral themes, the more I become absorbed with that kind of painting. And I begin to care less for those overblown nudes of Cabanel, for example." He paused thoughtfully.

"I count Jaquet along with him also. And there is Benjamin Constant, so highly praised, but so inexpressibly dry in his technique. And yet, I feel deeply for some artists' work, artists who do not even paint peasants, or pastoral themes, Raffaelli, for example, or Tissot. You will find as you keep looking, things will become clearer."

His words to me were like pebbles plopping into still water, the circle growing ever wider as new thoughts came to me. I began to digest glimmers of what he meant. When he spoke to me of his own pictures I sensed the deep feelings imbedded in his work. That heightened emotion sometimes erupted into fever-like animation, like the time he painted my aunt, but today he appeared calmer.

The canvas he was working on was simply a portion of the path winding through the gardens. But Vincent had infused life into the blue-black branches of the overhanging cypresses, into the tiny plants sheltering under the huge tree. To one side, two figures, a man and a woman, stood like lovers in contemplation on the path.

He imagined these gardens as "The Poet's Garden" recalling an article he had read on Dante and Petrarch and other Renaissance figures.

"You know, Minette, Petrarch lived quite near here, in Avignon, and it is easy to imagine him in a garden like this one, making his way over the flowery grass, sheltering from the sun under these gracious old trees."

Petrarch rang a distant bell from my school days. What a long

time, it seemed, since I had sat at a schoolroom desk. My mother
had insisted I go to school as long as possible, and I had been a
good student. I had always prided myself on getting my sums
right and on reading well.

Now I was grateful to Vincent for expanding my world, a world
that lately had been so crowded with hardship and work, I had
forgotten the simple joy of learning new things.

There were to be four garden pictures to decorate the rooms of
the Little Yellow House along with a series of sunflower paintings,
a painting of Vincent's bedroom and a portrait of Madame Roulin
rocking her baby's cradle. His enthusiasm infected me. Again the
thought came to me: he is more alive than anyone I have ever known.

Vincent talked on as he painted. I watched as he applied
viridian green, blue, both cobalt and Prussian blue, and chrome
yellow to his canvas, always painting boldly, assuredly. He told me
some of the garden pictures would decorate the spare bedroom,
and he hoped his friend Gauguin would occupy it, if he decided
to come to Arles.

"I wrote Gauguin of my Poet's Garden series," he said. "I told
him it was not Petrarch I recalled, rather it was Gauguin, the new
poet of the Midi in Arles. Gauguin, a great poet and painter who
would come to work with me."

As Vincent talked on about Gauguin's coming as though he
were a messiah of sorts, I understood how deeply he wished for a
companion, a soulmate, if you like, to come and work with him,
sharing successes and also disappointments. I watched the canvas
as the branches took shape, beds of orange geraniums blossomed
and the pair of lovers stood there, sharing a silent moment.

The picture was painted in a full impasto, very thickly, and as
often with him, looking directly at nature. Nature was Vincent's
starting point, although he freely altered what he saw to suit his
unique vision. Gauguin, he had told me many times, worked
differently, from his imagination. Silently I wondered how two
artists with such diverse attitudes to painting would get on,
although Vincent was so enthusiastic I did not voice my concerns.

*   *   *

For several days a new diner had been coming to the cafe. Young, tall, and neatly dressed, he spoke courteously and although he wore the clothing of a workman, his hands and fingernails were carefully cleaned. I noticed him because most of the diners were regulars, but I had not as yet waited on his table.

He was seated at his table at noontime when Charles, the house painter, approached him and asked if he might sit down. The young man nodded, smiling slightly, gesturing toward the other chair. Of course Edith began at once to flutter about the table. Charles proudly introduced her, letting it drop that they would be married in a fortnight. This I overheard as I went by carrying plates of stew to a table nearby.

For the first time I saw the stranger looking at me and I quickly lowered my gaze. What lovely green eyes he had! Then he smiled at me.

He left the cafe with Charles. Edith announced importantly that he was a joiner and that his name was Etienne Martin. He had only been in Arles for a short time working on the new municipal building. He came from Nimes.

*   *   *

When it became general knowledge that Edith and Charles were really going to be wed, my aunt sent me home to Saint Remy on the Sunday carrying a letter for my mother, in which she suggested that Colette come to Arles to work in the cafe, because an extra waitress would be needed to take Edith's place. I marveled at my aunt's ability to see every situation so clearly, and I applauded her loyalty to my mother who after all was only a sister-in-law and no blood kin.

The idea of Colette sharing my room and my work was not all that agreeable to me. Even though she was my sister, Colette, like Edith, was deceitful and a tale bearer. Had I not discovered this as we grew up together? Frankly, I did not look forward to her company, although I realized it would make life easier for my mother who could stay at home with Francine now as she handled the laundry business. As I had thought, my mother was overjoyed at the news.

But Colette would be a laggard and a slacker. I knew she would! She was happy to learn that she would be going out in the big, wide world, to Arles. Francine was pleased to see me, but my brothers were wrapped up in each other, as usual. I spent most of my time with Francine, telling her about the artist I had met who promised to tell me about his painting techniques and to talk with me about books he was reading.

"He has even loaned me one of his books about French painters," I said. "It has lovely pictures in it." I told her about going to watch Vincent painting in the public gardens, of the warm, sunny colors that gave the pictures a feeling of happiness, the figures of the lovers and the blue green branches of the cypress. I told her about the Little Yellow House and its beautifully colored rooms. She hung on every word, and talking about Vincent pleased me like nothing else could.

As for my mother, she had begun the slow process of healing after my father's sudden death. That she had been able to keep going and to provide for her family was a victory of sorts, for she had been left with very little when my father died. And now, against all odds, she had succeeded, with the prospect of two of us bringing in francs on a regular basis, in addition to our room and board. My brothers had accepted their responsibilities as men, even though they were still boys. She had every right to feel proud.

Only the slight cloud of Francine's delicate health darkened the horizon, and I truly believed she looked stronger and healthier since I had been sending along the extra francs from the laundry work I was doing. My mother proudly told me she was saving up to buy a cow, then they could have fresh milk and butter and cheese. So I returned to Arles, telling Aunt Titi that my family was well, and that Colette was ready to come as soon as she was needed.

Tuesday I set out for the wash house carrying the baskets when I was met by Etienne on a dead trot from his building site. "I've come to carry your baskets to the wash house!" Surprised but pleased he had taken the trouble, I handed them over and as we walked, he asked me about my visit home. He said he had never been to Saint Remy and wondered what the town was like. He added that he would like to visit it someday.

"It is a small village with one main street lined with plane trees which is rather pretty, especially in the autumn, when the leaves turn a wonderful golden color. There is not much to it, really, with olive groves surrounding the town."

"Ah, then it is like some of the streets where I come from, Nimes, with plane trees giving a wonderful shade in summer. Nimes is a beautiful place."

"How did you happen to come to Arles?" I asked.

"Like everyone else, I suppose. For a chance to see a little of the world, to earn some money." The honest green eyes under a fringe of straight brown hair regarded me as we walked. He was very polite and did not ask me questions about my life. Time for that later, I thought.

"Would you walk out with me some evening after the cafe closes, Minette?" he said suddenly, taking me by surprise. He stopped walking, turned to me and waited. The green eyes, I noticed, deepened in the shade.

"I might," I answered saucily, "if I'm free!" I didn't want to encourage him too much. I was mainly interested in Vincent. But Etienne's thoughtfulness in carrying the baskets impressed me. He was on my mind as I beat and rinsed the clothes. He was different from most of the men who took their meals at the cafe, not startlingly different like Vincent of course, but thoughtful and considerate and, well, handsome.

CHAPTER SEVEN

Vincent had worked the past week painting portraits of the Postman Roulin and his wife. The *mistral*, that cold, northern wind of Provence, had screeched and howled all weekend. Now it was over, and Vincent was impatient to get back outdoors to paint. He still had another garden picture to finish, this one in front of a rather poor cottage on the outskirts of town. Would I like to go along?

"I'll have to meet you after the noonday diners have left," I said, "but I'd love to come." It was about half past two when I set out. The summer had turned glorious in Arles and the surrounding area. Now we were coming into the harvest with long, golden days of brilliant yellow sun and golden grain waving in the fields. I knew my brothers were working frantically in Saint Remy to harvest the grain before rain. The harvest held so much promise for all of them, I thought wistfully. If the fields looked anything like the fields around Arles, there would be an abundant crop.

Following Vincent's direction and remembering to wear Aunt Titi's straw hat, I walked quickly, following the road toward Montmajour abbey. The garden, at the edge of town, was an humble thing, but a monument to beauty. Seeds had been sown with great skill and lavishness, and everything had flourished. "Each in its own kind to replenish the earth," ran through my head, a half-remembered Bible verse that came to mind as I gazed at the spectacle. Hollyhocks, larkspur, poppies and zinnias, snapdragons and marigolds and clove-scented pinks happily lived together in that garden, with bright nasturtiums scrambling among the rocks and sandy patches near the road.

It was a garden of profusion, an English style garden I learned later from Vincent. I spotted him in the wide-brimmed straw hat, almost hidden by the wealth of blooms. He was busy painting the foreground in some detail.

I asked him about the Roulin portraits. "They are finished!" he said happily, "and I am pleased. I would like for you to become better acquainted with the Roulins, Minette. They are a perfect example of the blissful married state. If only all married couples could be as they!" His eyes took on a faraway look. "Then their children are a jolly lot, and of course, the new baby Marcelle. She is barely a month old."

"Vincent," I asked boldly, "how is it that you have never married? You seem envious of the Roulin's happiness." Vincent put down his brush and turned to me.

"Minette, I am going to tell you something nobody in the whole world knows about me, except Theo, of course. I am thirty-five years old, Minette. When I was sent to London to work for my uncle in his art gallery, I fell in love with the daughter of my landlady. Her name was Ursula Loy. She rejected me.

"Then, when I returned to Etten to live with my parents I fell in love with a cousin, Kee Voss, a young widow with a child. She rejected me. That was in 1881. In 1882 I took in a fallen woman in Antwerp where I was working, a woman with a child. I would have married her, her name was Sien, but my brother pointed out the disgrace it would bring down on my family if I did such a thing. He was right, of course.

"In 1884 I went to live with my parents again, this time at Nuenen where they had moved. There I fell in love with a neighbor, Margot Begemann. She attempted suicide, so I stopped seeing her because the family objected.

"Now painting has become by obsession," he said, taking up the brush. "My pictures will have to be my children. Who could live with me? Clearly, it is not meant for me to enter the married state."

"No, Vincent, surely not!" I cried, my heart weeping for all the unhappiness and disappointments he had suffered. "You must not give up. Many men have found a helpmate, a life's companion, when they were older than you."

"Ah, Minette, you almost give me hope."

"None of us should be without it!" I said passionately. "Vincent," I said wildly, struck with a sudden thought, "I could work for you as your housekeeper, keep things tidy and get your meals on time." Perhaps this occurred to me because he had told me he often forgot to eat for long stretches of time when he was especially busy working. But he saw right through my impetuous suggestion, saw it for what it was, a desperate bid for his attentions.

"Stop!" He held up one hand in a joking manner, "Your temptations will surely overwhelm me! Seriously, Minette, you know how fond I am of you, why there is no one in Arles whom I value more. But listen, there is my dark side. Because you have not seen it does not mean it is non-existent. It is very real, and not a pretty sight. I value you too much to encourage you in any closer relationship with me.

"That is why I do not ask you to walk with me after closing time. Or to visit me alone again in the Little Yellow House. I might let my feelings overwhelm me and sweep us along torrents that would make it impossible to save ourselves. Then there would be the inevitable recrimination and regret." I kept silent, but I despaired at his words. It was about as plain as the nose on my face, Vincent did not want us to become closer.

Several days after that amazing talk with Vincent, I was still sorting out my feelings for him. I had supposed he was innocently unaware of my love for him. On the contrary, he had known precisely of my feelings, perceived the love I felt for him almost before I myself was aware of it. How neatly and tactfully he had sidestepped any deeper development of affection between us! Now all was in limbo. I felt a disappointment and a frustration unlike anything I'd experienced before.

This was the state of things when Etienne asked me to walk with him after the cafe closed that night. It was Thursday and my back ached from all the ironing I'd done that afternoon, but I agreed because I wanted to learn more about him. He piqued my interest, in spite of myself. I wanted to know him better.

There were a lot of young people on the streets as we made our way toward the arena. The bars and some of the cafes were still open, spilling out a golden, phosphorous light on to the pavements. We came upon Edmond and Hubert Lantier, Aunt Titi's nephews, making their way toward the ancient structure. It was the scene of bull fights now, on Sunday afternoons. I introduced Etienne and the four of us continued walking together.

Edmond and Hubert kept us laughing. They complemented each other, each led in to the other's jokes. But still, they seemed very young to me. Actually, the three men were about the same age, around twenty years. Etienne, however, seemed older to me. Perhaps it was because he was more serious.

Edmond began singing to us a song of a forlorn sailor who misplaced his ship and spent the night looking for it as he became the worse for wear from drink. There was a lot of laughter. I realized that I was having a good time. Etienne joined in the chorus as we picked our way over the pointed cobblestones. As we turned into the darkened arena, the moon came from behind a cloud and I could see courting couples everywhere in the shadows. This was a sight I'd never seen before. Silly of me not to realize . . .

I suppose it was inescapable. Where else was there privacy except in the open fields outside of town? Voices were subdued and in the moonlight I could just make out forms of half a dozen couples standing wrapped in passionate embraces as we passed by. Somewhat embarrassed, we hurried on, turning to go back out to the street, but not before I glimpsed a familiar blond head bent over a small woman, his arms locked around her, his body pushing against her in the most primitive way. Van Gogh!

In one hand he clutched a wine bottle. I felt sickened at the sight, betrayed. This bestial, pulsing creature could surely not be the same gentle man I knew. So proper . . . speaking to me of married love, of pride of family. Why, the simple animals of the forests were more forthright, I thought wildly. At least they did not seek their pleasures in a drunken stupor. A wave of shame swept over me. I was afraid he would see me. I needn't have worried, for he was far too occupied. Disgust filled me.

Etienne, not recognizing anyone he knew but embarrassed, propelled me rapidly out into the street. We caught up with the Lantier brothers again and completed our stroll together. Except for the shock of seeing Vincent, it had been a pleasant evening. I could not stop thinking about what I had seen as I exchanged goodbyes with Etienne at the cafe door.

The very next day Vincent came to the cafe at noonday, asking me to walk to Montmajour abbey with him that afternoon where he intended to paint the ruins. But I begged off, pretending a headache and wearily went to my room to brood, thankful Edith and Gisele were out.

As I lay alone on my cot I let anger take over from the shock of the night before. How dare he come running to me after disporting himself so for all the world to see! But then it was just what had been said of him—two separate personalities, the wolf and the lamb. My thoughts flashed back to Mauricette and her friend at the wash house . . . to Aunt Titi who told me what the Prefect had said. My cheeks burned. He had played me the fool, all right. Had he appeared at that moment, I would have told him off, then and there. But I discovered a part of me still pitied the tortured human being who had failed at so many things and had been cast off by so many people.

*   *   *

Edith's final day at the cafe arrived before she and Charles would walk to the church to be married, then travel by wagon to

Fontvielle nearby where her parents owned a farm. There the wedding feast would take place. After a few days the couple would return to Arles to look for a place to live, temporarily lodging in Charles' rooms in the Rue Lepic.

"It is far too small," Edith complained. "We will be unable to breathe, should you come to call. But never fear, we will find a larger place, then you may visit."

Gisele and I listened in silence as she talked on, not wishing to pay her a call at all. We were helping her fold her belongings into a worn valise covered in dark red tapestry roses. She had become impossible since her engagement, treating us as inferiors because she was to be married and we had no prospects. It did not worry me, but I could see in Gisele's face she was hurting.

I fingered the lovely white nightgown with row after row of lace which Aunt Titi had given Edith. What a beautiful thing! Unbidden, a horrid image of Vincent and his woman, writhing in the arena, surfaced in my mind. Would I never be free of that hated memory?

The departure of Edith meant the arrival of Colette with her tossing black curls and her assured ways. With a sigh I reckoned poor Gisele and I were out of one pickle into another!

I had not held a private conversation with Vincent since the awful night at the arena, but I was getting to know Etienne quite well. He liked to tell me about the family farm, and I discovered I could talk of my family and my father's death. I realized that with Vincent, we never seemed to talk of my life, only what had happened in his. I learned that Etienne's mother managed the prosperous family farm outside Nimes. His two brothers helped run it. That is why Etienne had left, to strike out on his own and make his way.

My thoughts continued to ramble as always when I was at the ironing board. I enjoyed the Thursday afternoons in the big kitchen, smelling the freshly ironed linens as I worked with the two flat irons and Monsieur Raspail read the daily paper sitting on a little bench outside the kitchen door. The stacks of freshly ironed napkins mounted. Aunt Titi was upstairs resting and Colette, who had arrived that morning, was in our room with Gisele arranging her things. The kitchen door opened a crack and Vincent came in looking agitated.

"You have been avoiding me, Minette," he said in a low voice. "I have come to find out what is the matter. What about our talks of books and paintings? Have you lost interest? Why have you been so cool toward me?"

I stood there, careful to rest the iron on its stand, and looked at him for a full minute before I spoke. "You have been busy, too busy to have any thought of me," I answered shortly.

"Well, yes, I have been busy, painting every day until the sun drops, driven to go on as something is ending, when the summer trickles away and the shorter days are already beginning. I feel I must capture what I can, in the time I have." What did he mean by that I thought?

"Also," he went on, "I have been writing many letters to my brother and to my friend Gauguin in Brittany. It looks as though he will be arriving, maybe in October."

"How very nice for you," I answered coldly. "Then you will have company in your evenings." I wondered if he would notice the irony in my voice.

"You have heard something about me, or seen something, What is it?" His voice was blunt, the words angry. Silently I marveled at his intuition as I looked at his eyes, burning like blue fire.

"I had heard things before, Vincent, which I believed to be gossip or vicious rumors which were untrue. I did not believe them. This time I have seen for myself, with my own eyes. Disgusting things." There, I had said it. No more beating around the bush.

"So now you know what I mean when I say dark currents course through me, or when I tell you I am tormented by two people, each one vying for control within me." Vincent paused.

"Yes, I admit it," he went on. "I have been to the arena with women, and I have been drunk there. And I will probably go there again to find a kind of release in such degradation. I will take with me some woman who sells her soul for a few francs, or maybe like me she is one of the lonely ones, left out at life's table. What joy we find briefly in each other's bodies is only a sop to a yearning to be like normal people, living normal lives." I stood there mute, desperately wishing I were somewhere else, that this trunk of horrors had not been opened.

"So I do not deny this, Minette. Nor do I apologize. Like the mulatto who can never pass as white, or the Jew who can never pose as a Christian, I am one of the cursed and the damned, compelled to carry a cross every day of my life until death releases me. It is how I am made."

I was crying now, tears flowing down my cheeks. Poor creature, poor wronged creature. I cursed the world that had made Vincent and hated myself for the revulsion I felt. I did not think I could ever forgive Vincent for what I had seen with my own eyes, but having listened to him, I could not blame him either. Without another word, he turned and left.

CHAPTER EIGHT

The tables of the cafe bloomed with vases of giant sunflowers. I could hardly believe my eyes, coming downstairs for breakfast one morning. Aunt Titi, sipping *cafe au lait*, feasted on the glorious display. There must have been three dozen huge sunflower blossoms in six or eight vases.

"It takes the breath away, eh Minette? See what our painter friend has lavished upon us!"

"Not my painter, Aunt," I answered quickly. "It is your portrait he painted."

She shrugged. "Whatever the gods give us, we accept. Not ours to question. Do not be too hard on Vincent. Whatever he has done to displease you, he does not deserve it."

So she had noticed the friction between us. I wondered how she would feel if she had seen what I saw. I marveled at Aunt Titi's ability to sense, if not guess, the truth of every situation so finely tuned were her perceptions. I had told her nothing of that fateful scene in the arena, but she had sensed something amiss between the two of us.

"Where on earth did he find all of those sunflowers?" I asked.

"He brought them in fresh from the field this morning, given to him by a farmer for a small sketch he made of his wife. There are many more, I believe, set up in the Little Yellow House. He is going to paint sunflower pictures to decorate the rooms. I understand Gauguin's arrival is something of a sure thing."

So many! I gasped in spite of myself. If drink and carousing with women did not kill Vincent, he would surely die of overwork. And I knew he did not eat properly. He made his own meals to save money most of the time, but, remembering the loaf and the end of cheese I'd seen in his kitchen, I knew it was a makeshift business, those meals.

"Truly they are magnificent, Aunt," I said, looking at the sunflowers dominating the cafe, their spectacular golden heads proudly upright in the morning sun. "You must have been hard pressed to find containers for all of them."

"Oh, Vincent helped me. In fact, he insisted on arranging them. You never saw such a fuss over every flower, every stem, every leaf."

"So he will finish the paintings before Gauguin arrives." I shook my head thinking,and he will forget to eat most of the time.

"Oh yes," she said, "He paints so rapidly. You remember my portrait of course. I promised him we would come and see when all is finished in the Little Yellow House." Not if I can help it, I thought. But I said nothing.

Why I mused, shaking out freshly washed and ironed cloths over the tables for lunch, couldn't I get over Vincent's behavior at the arena? I admit that in the beginning, when I first met him, I had daydreamed about the two of us being lovers, eventually husband and wife in some fantasyland. But I never really thought it would happen. Our worlds were too far apart.

I was a peasant at heart, never very far removed from the land and the business of getting enough to eat. I knew there was no chance of a life for Vincent and me together. I was a poor waitress, turning over everything I made to help my family. And Vincent? He was committed to sending his paintings to his brother. In exchange, the brother provided him with enough money to live on. There was little more than enough for food, canvases and paints, certainly not enough money to keep a wife.

No, I hadn't supposed in my heart of hearts we could ever be together. But I had loved the pedestal Vincent put me on, and it hurt to discover he had toppled from the pedestal where I'd placed him. That was the nub of the matter. That was the reason I could not truly forgive him. But what was that my wise aunt had just said? Something about being accepting of what the gods give us? Not ours to question?

After finishing my work I looked around the room. What an amazing display. It was as though the sunflowers had become beings in their own right, bringing a new dimension of beauty into the world. Those humble flowers of the field assumed the cloak of refinement in that plain little cafe dining room. Never had I seen anything more beautiful. Where my aunt or I would have massed the blooms in fewer vases, Vincent gave each flower its own space, and by doing so gave it a worth of its own.

When the diners arrived for the noon meal there was a lot of joking and laughter. There was no doubt in anyone's mind who had brought all those sunflowers. I was sure of that. Vincent in their minds was the town's odd man. Some of them probably thought he was a little mad. Of art they understood nothing, so they could not know how well he practiced his craft. But at the same time they knew he was not skimpy about things that mattered. They sensed, as could I, that he had a tremendous appetite for life.

*   *   *

When Colette first arrived I was told to "break her in" by my aunt. Getting her accustomed to the routine of the cafe went surprisingly well. She responded smartly to the crisp, no nonsense standards of Aunt Titi and she did a good job. I was actually proud of my fifteen year old sister. She took orders carefully and was neat in her serving. No one brought their orders out of the kitchen more swiftly or responded to requests quicker than Colette. And she seemed to have outgrown the sly ways I remembered at home. I supposed that she also had changed a lot since my father's death.

It had brought us more responsibility, and more maturity. I had said nothing to her yet about helping with the laundry. That could wait. She might even want to help, once she settled in.

"Who is that good looking man who follows you with his eyes every evening?" she asked as we waited for the diners to arrive. I shrugged, knowing she meant Etienne.

"The one you said who carried the laundry baskets for you last Tuesday," Colette added and I knew I would have to tell her. She would not stop asking.

"Only Etienne Martin," I answered as casually as I could. "He is a joiner from Nimes working on the new municipal building. He is just a friend."

"Hmmm," she answered. "He watches you the whole time. Anyone can tell he is sweet on you. Don't you know?"

"No, and I still don't. Come on, Aunt will be cross if we lag about!"

But Colette was irrepressible and her common sense and good humor made the customers like her. She soon had pairs of admiring eyes following her as she served, but her favorites were Aunt Titi's nephews, Edmond and Hubert Lantier. Before she arrived they came for meals occasionally. Now they were regulars every evening. Sometimes with Gisele and Etienne we all walked briskly on some of the main streets after the cafe closed in the evenings. But Etienne avoided the arena and I was grateful for that.

*   *   *

The sunflowers lasted several days. Then we had to throw them out. "This means Van Gogh has probably finished his sunflower paintings," Aunt Titi said as we cleaned the vases. Such a horrid smell. The fetid water and slimy, decaying stems and leaves were repugnant. I knew he couldn't be working with the flowers anymore.

I was reminded of the flowers' fragile, ephemeral aspect. But never, if I lived to be a hundred I thought, would I ever forget the dazzling spectacle of their beauty in that room. Time has proved my prediction right.

"So," Aunt continued, "I am going to prepare a cassoulet of beef and vegetables to take to him along with an apple tart to thank him for his kindness. He always seems to look hungry to me. We will take it over before midday and can have a quick look at his Little Yellow House. We'll be back in time for the lunch service, but I'll tell Colette and Gisele to be on their toes, just in case we are a minute late."

Arguing with my aunt was never very successful, so I saved myself the trouble of trying to beg off. In all honesty I wanted very much to see what Vincent had accomplished since my first impromptu visit alone. Thank goodness Aunt knew nothing of that!

We left as soon as the dinner was ready, the cassoulet and the tart wrapped carefully and placed in separate baskets lined with cloths to preserve the heat. This time Place Lamartine was teeming with life. Children skipped on the sidewalks and I recognized Mauricette and the other woman from the wash house gossiping together as they watched their children playing. Neither seemed to recognize me, but they bowed respectfully toward us as we passed.

As my aunt had predicted, all traces of the sunflowers had vanished. In their place were the drying canvases ranged around the small studio. The flowers were complete; he had captured them before they faded, but the containers, various crocks and pitchers, were only roughly sketched in. These he had been working on when we arrived.

He thanked us effusively for the dishes, eyeing them hungrily. I felt sure Vincent had vaulted out of bed early that morning and had gone to work painting without making his breakfast. Oh, Vincent, I thought sadly, how you need looking after!

Aunt insisted he continue to work. We could stay only a few moments and we would like to watch him if we might? He was enormously pleased, immediately propping two canvases against the wall and seating us in the room's two chairs. He moved to the easel and began working on a blue pottery jug holding several finished sunflowers.

"Yes, I have been hard at it," he said, "with all the enthusiasm of a Marseillais eating bouillabaisse. Never have I painted so many studies of the same motif! Of course they vary. One has only three flowers, one a bud, the other gone to seed. They all will decorate this studio when they are finished. I want to make the whole thing a symphony in blue and yellow. You will see that these canvases catch the eye. They are the kind of paintings that rather change in character, and take on a richness the longer you look at them." He continued to talk as he worked.

"The artist Jeanin has claimed the peony as his own. The hollyhock belongs to Quost, but now, I believe the sunflower will become my own." He had no idea, of course, how true would be those words.

I noted that on one of the jugs of simple brown and cream color, he had painted "Vincent" on the band of cream. That signature seemed poignant, child-like to me.

I had brought along Vincent's book by the de Goncourt brothers, and he insisted on loaning me another book, a volume on the painter Millet by Sensier. Now I knew Millet was a painter Vincent admired most—he had made many copies and variations from Millet's work for many years.

"I should not take it, Vincent, you might need to consult it for your painting," I said.

"All the more reason why I want you to read it! So you can see what inspires me! Remember I told you once how I loved best of all artists who devote themselves to pastoral work? Certainly Millet is at the top of that list." And so I carried the book under my arm as Aunt Titi and I left.

"What do you think this painter Gauguin will be like?" she asked as we walked briskly toward the cafe.

"Of course, Vincent thinks Gauguin is the greatest man on earth and can do no wrong. That is what he says to me, anyway.

Vincent is a hopeless idealist and I am not so sure all will be well. I know Gauguin asked Vincent to approach his brother Theo to persuade him to support him in the way he supports Vincent, by sending a monthly stipend in exchange for pictures, before they are sold."

"That would be quite a drain on the brother, one would think," Aunt murmured thoughtfully. "Is the brother older than Vincent?"

"No, younger by four years."

"So, he is not earning so much perhaps, as a junior member of the firm," Aunt Titi spoke carefully. "And this Gauguin, is he a single man?"

"No, married with six children. The wife returned to her people in Copenhagen with all the children when Gauguin could no longer support them. He is in Brittany now, painting I believe."

"Oh, la, la," my aunt clicked her tongue. "Trouble ahead."

CHAPTER NINE

Out of the blue Vincent came to me at the cafe and asked permission to paint my portrait. A month earlier I would have jumped over the moon with joy. Now, however, my heart was heavy. After all that had happened I was disillusioned with Vincent, at least I no longer thought of him as a lover.

"Of course she will sit for you," said Aunt Titi, who was nearby. "Of course, Monsieur Van Gogh. Can you work Wednesday afternoons when Minette has time off?"

"Indeed yes, Madame. And would you permit her to sit in my studio? My paints are immediately at hand, the light is perfect. It will be much easier that way."

"But of course," answered my aunt. As yet I had not said one word. "That can be arranged. Of course, she must be accompanied. Either I or perhaps Colette will come with her. Minette," she turned to me, "What should you wear? I think the new rose print would be best, what do you think, Monsieur?" Unwilling to provoke an argument and secretly flattered, I agreed with the plans and the date was set for the following Wednesday afternoon. And yes, I wore the rose print.

It came as a surprise to me that Colette disapproved of this arrangement. "That man is like a loaded cannon all set to explode," she said. "You really should not give him the time of day! What will Etienne think?"

"It's not Etienne's business, and you are wrong, Vincent wouldn't hurt a fly!" My answer was quick and peppery. Suddenly I realized how quickly I had leapt to Vincent's defense. "Wouldn't any girl like to have her portrait painted by an artist who will one day be famous?"

"Humph!" Colette snorted. "And pigs will fly! Oh well, do as you like. It doesn't matter to me! But take care Etienne doesn't lose interest."

Gisele dropped off to sleep early that night as we sank down in our cots, and I asked Colette why she disliked Vincent so much. I was beginning to value her opinions; she had grown up so much in the past year, and most of all, her deceitful ways seemed to be a thing of the past. I admitted to myself that I had possibly misjudged Colette.

"Why don't you like Vincent, Colette? After all, you've hardly met him."

She thought for a minute before she answered, her forehead screwed into a frown. "I don't dislike him. I have a feeling that you two have been pretty close. Am I right?" I nodded. "But things are not going so well for you now, yes?" Again I nodded.

"Then leave it, Minette. Maybe it was not meant to be. Gisele tells me he has never sold a painting, not one. And that his brother has to support him. What kind of a catch is that, Minette, I ask you? You'd find yourself in the same boat as *Maman*, forced to work twice as hard to support a family. Is that what you really want? Believe me, Minette, I've seen how hard life can really be! Me, I'm looking for a rich husband! At least someone who can provide a comfortable living for me and the children we might have. Van Gogh is a loser."

Trust Colette to give me the world's view, I thought, but I was surprised at her depth of feeling. Our father's untimely death had changed all of us in many ways. For all her flippant talk, Colette, who had to grow up very fast, possessed a high degree of common sense. Yet, a part of her childhood had been taken away from her,

I thought. Her opinion of Vincent had the weight of logic. And I dropped off to sleep still thinking of what she had said.

*   *   *

One night Gisele did not come home. As it grew later and later, well past midnight, I began to worry. Colette of course was sleeping like a contented puppy so I could not share my anxieties. Gisele had said she was going out for a breath of fresh air "with the others", but I had not noticed anyone else around when she left. Colette came in just after half-past eleven after strolling with the Lantier brothers. I didn't even ask about Gisele. Surely she will show up soon, I thought.

When I heard the old clock in the hall strike two I shook Colette gently until she awoke. "Gisele hasn't come in yet, it's two o'clock!"

Colette was awake in an instant. "But I saw her just before I came back myself!"

"Who was she with?"

"No one especially. You know how she drifts along with a group. They were all together, I remember."

"Then we'd better wake Aunt Titi," I said.

"No! What can she do now? Better we wait and tell her the first thing in the morning." Colette was right, I realized. Besides, Gisele might still show up.

But as I awoke when the first streaky pink appeared in our window, her cot was still empty. I knew we had to tell my aunt.

"Silly girl!" were my aunt's first words. "She will get her throat slit if she is not careful, meandering about in the black of night!" But she dressed quickly and after a cup of coffee, she questioned Colette closely about the party of strollers. Then she set down her cup. "I'll go at once to the police."

*   *   *

Gisele's disappearance quickly became the talk of the cafe.

Because all the young men of the party were accounted for and none claimed to have been with her, her whereabouts remained a mystery. The police had scoured the arena, the Alyscamps, the public gardens, but they turned up nothing. No bodies had been retrieved from the Rhone. Gisele seemed to have vanished without a trace.

Colette and I had no real difficulty in taking over her serving chores. Gisele had been inefficient at her job, although even-tempered and willing. She was simply slow. It was disturbing to be confronted by her clothing, her comb and brush, the gingham nightgown she wore hanging on a peg behind the door. And her empty cot.

Aunt Titi shook her head as we made our way to the Little Yellow House on the Wednesday. "Poor, poor Gisele. I cannot get it out of my head that something dreadful has happened to her."

"Didn't she have any family, Aunt?"

"The Cure had suggested to me that she might work at the cafe. She came from the Sisters at the abbey at Montpelier, and I never knew anything about her, where she was born and so on. Apparently she was an orphan."

Vincent met us at the door of the Little Yellow House. Right away I knew something was wrong. His face was a picture, a mingling of embarrassment and dread. Something was weighing on his mind. When we were settled in his studio, he turned gravely toward my aunt.

"Madame Ginoux, I have information that I believe you would like to hear." He fidgeted with the tubes of paint, preparing to put color on his palette. His eyes were downcast. What could be worrying him?

"Oh yes?" said my aunt, settling into the brown chair in the studio, glad to be off her feet after our walk.

"I know where Gisele has gone," he said simply, his voice low. I hardly caught the words, they were spoken so softly.

But my aunt had no difficulty hearing. "You what? Then where is she?"

"She has gone to live at the *Maison de Tolerance.*"

The words hit us like an exploding rocket. If he had told us she had been carried away by a handsome prince on a white horse, I could not have been more surprised.

It took my aunt a moment to recover and to restrain herself from blurting out, "How did you know?" Instead, she asked, "Are you certain she has gone to the brothel?"

"I am certain. I have spoken to her." He said it honestly and unconditionally. How like you, Vincent, to put your head into the lion's mouth! Silently I applauded his courage.

"Well, really!" spluttered my aunt. "I am not pleased to learn that one of my serving girls has run off to a brothel. I will have you know, Monsieur, I run a decent cafe. There is no hanky—panky at my cafe, I can tell you!"

"Of course, Madame Ginoux," Vincent said firmly. "No one doubts that either you or your young ladies are of the highest moral caliber."

"May I ask what she said to you? We have been greatly worried at her disappearance. We feared she had met with some horrible accident, or that an abduction had taken place."

"I understand your concerns," he replied. "I tried my best to urge her to come to you, make a clean breast of what has happened, to ask your forgiveness for any worry you have been caused."

"Any worry? Well, yes. she caused that, all right!" My aunt's voice was full of righteous indignation.

"She promised me she would go and see you," Vincent said. "I had hoped this might have occurred by now. However, I am sure she is finding it very difficult to summon the necessary courage to face you . . . . It is difficult for me just to tell you!"

I felt pangs of sympathy for Vincent and poor Gisele. If I had to face Aunt Titi with such horrifying news, I would be quaking in my boots, that was certain. My aunt shook her head.

"That hussy! That brazen, immoral hussy! To think, working in my cafe, sharing a room with two of my own nieces! She must surely realize she is ruining herself, going to a place like that! We must try to get her out!"

"I do not believe that would be wise," said Vincent, speaking very softly.

"You surely do not think she should remain in such a depraved, immoral environment? Are you mad?" Did I imagine it, or did Vincent flinch ever so slightly at her words?

"Madame, when I discovered Gisele, and I hope you understand how it pains me to reveal my, ah, weakness to you and Minette, she had been there two days. I spoke to her at once and tried to talk to her as a brother or as a father, pointing out the pitfalls of her actions. She is a very unhappy woman, Madame. She realizes she is not only lacking somewhat in intelligence, but her appearance is also somewhat, ah, unfortunate. She is not an attractive looking person. And yet, she is human.

"She longs for a family to which she can attach herself, something she says she never had. She believes she has now found a family of sorts in the community she has joined. Who are we to deny her this? I certainly cannot urge anyone to follow my path! But I can show compassion and kindness to her, and I will not condemn her! And you should not either, Madame. We all are, I repeat, all, children of one God." Here the blue eyes caught fire and his features grew intense.

I knew the gleam in those icy blue eyes meant Vincent's temper was rising and I hoped and prayed Aunt Titi would conceal her outraged feelings and at least try for a calm discourse with Vincent.

I should have known she would read the situation like a familiar map! At once she acquiesced, thanking Vincent solemnly for the information and graciously accepting his offer to take Gisele's belongings to her new home. As to Vincent's obvious knowledge of the house of ill fame, Aunt Titi knew when to cut her losses and remain silent. But I knew on our way home I would get an earful of outrage and hurt pride, an outpouring of indignation that she should have lost one of her employees to a brothel!

After such a dismal beginning, the sitting, surprisingly, went well enough. Vincent liked the color of the rose print dress I wore, commenting on its suitability for my dark coloring. My skin was coffee-tinted, darker than the pale rose of the dress, and my eyes gray, my hair ash brown, "a real girl of this country" Vincent proclaimed. "Your straight nose is pure Greek," he said, and I was pleased.

The background for my figure was unusual, completely covered in tiny green leaves. Wallpaper, I supposed is what he had in mind. To me it looked like I was sitting next to a budding fig tree, my figure almost merging with hundreds of tiny green leaves.

Having Vincent paint my portrait lifted my spirits. I was secretly pleased with the quiet image of a shy-looking girl wearing a dress with a tight, high necked bodice which showed off a trim, smallish bosom in a very flattering way. That is how the portrait was emerging.

"You look like spring itself," my aunt said, looking at the canvas as we prepared to leave. "So fresh and innocent." I blushed thinking how shocked she would be had she known I had paid a visit alone to the Little Yellow House. As it was, she parted with Vincent on the most cordial of terms. We would return the following Wednesday, she promised, when Vincent planned to finish the portrait.

"Well, and what do you think of Gisele?" she asked as we walked away from the Little Yellow House toward the cafe.

"I, I don't know, Aunt," I answered uncertainly. "At least we know she is safe and hasn't been murdered."

"Humph! As if life in a place like that isn't dying a death of sorts!"

"But Aunt, maybe it is as Vincent said. When you are left out in everything—family, friends, good looks, intelligence, one might become desperate for something to belong to, for friendship with other women." But Aunt Titi would have none of it.

"How can you even think of such a thing, Minette? She will be old and used up, ready for humanity's scrap heap, in five years, if she isn't dead from disease. I accept that Monsieur Van Gogh is a genius in his art, give him that. But he is a dangerous man! Dangerous in his ideas, not that I believe he could ever harm anyone, but did you see the look that came into his eyes? When I spoke up, he quickly changed into a completely different person!"

I had to agree with her. I had seen it with my own eyes, how Vincent changed so quickly into a more threatening and sinister personality. I thought of this as Aunt Titi gave me more warnings about watching my step with Van Gogh. Not that I was likely to run off the rails, with both Aunt Titi and Colette pulling me back from the brink of disaster!

"Yes," she said, almost talking to herself, "I believe he could be dangerous, very dangerous indeed. Take heed, Minette. Don't ever fail to be on your guard with Monsieur Van Gogh!"

Now that there was the business of Gisele to occupy Vincent, he would probably be painting her next, yet even as I thought it, I knew he would not. But a tiny voice inside me asked if perhaps, just perhaps, loneliness had driven Gisele to the brothel as Vincent suggested. Had Edith, Colette, Aunt Titi and I failed her?

Arriving back at the cafe, Aunt Titi and I went to my room and together we gathered Gisele's things into a small, pathetic bundle so Vincent could collect them. As we were finishing the job, the Prefect called in to tell Aunt Titi the news of Gisele's whereabouts. She had come to register herself as was the law's requirement in Arles, he said.

"And how did she seem?" I heard Aunt Titi ask from my listening post at the top of the stairs. She did not reveal that we had received the news earlier, from Vincent.

"Ahem, well, she seemed normal," answered the Prefect carefully, his honesty preventing him from making the poor girl sound repentant, as he surely knew Aunt longed to hear.

"Poor lost soul," murmured my aunt as she climbed the stairs. "She always liked sugared almonds. I will put a sack of them into her valise."

CHAPTER TEN

As my disillusionment with Vincent grew, so did my friendship with Etienne. Being around him made me feel happy in a contented sort of way. His presence was not exhilarating, he made no demands, but he had earned my respect. He looked a fine figure of a man. Carrying my laundry baskets, bringing bouquets of flowers for me occasionally, these things were pleasing to me. When we went out walking in the evenings he was unfailingly courteous and correct, yet I was sure I was special to him. Hadn't Colette picked up on that early on? But he had never spoken to me of his feelings.

So I was taken with surprise when Colette came in one evening after walking with Edmond and Hubert and told me Etienne was walking with someone else! She was the new girl serving at the baker's shop where we went each day for fresh bread. Suzette was her name.

Pretty in an ordinary way, I thought spitefully. Wavy brown hair pulled severely back and tied with a ribbon. And an outstanding figure showing beneath her revealing blouse and dark skirts. I admitted that. I could see why Etienne would notice. But why, when I was sure he cared for me most of all?

The most disturbing questions rose in my mind. Had I been

so blinded by Vincent that I failed to make myself attentive to Etienne? Guiltily I thought of the time spent stewing and fretting over Vincent and his problems, how I frequently spent time with him, watching him paint, how he always claimed my attention when he appeared at the cafe. Now I realized that this would be off-putting to any suitor, certainly to a calm, even-tempered man like Etienne.

My feelings for Vincent had reached an impasse. I had known this for some time. Now I began to ponder just what my feelings for Etienne Martin were—and how I could begin to reclaim his affection.

*   *   *

"How would you like to give a hand with the laundry?" I asked Colette as we placed clean cloths over the tables before the midday meal.

"I wondered when you would ask," she laughed. "I suppose I must, so *Maman* will receive a good report when you next go to St. Remy!" She winked at me.

"I am still worrying about whether or not they will be able to cope next winter," I said, thinking not only of the lack of money, but of Francine's delicate health.

"Oh pooh," answered Colette in a bored voice. "Of course they'll be all right. You worry too much, Minette! By the way, I saw Gisele yesterday."

"Good heavens, where?"

"She was crossing the road with a dozen *baguettes*. She'd been to the baker for their daily order I guess."

"How did she look?"

"Same as always, really. But come to think, there was a little spring in her step I'd not seen before. She wasn't cowed or bowed down, you know. I think she is a sort of errand girl, a maid maybe. I don't think she is one of the . . . hostesses." As Colette searched for the right word, we dissolved into fits of giggles.

"Why ever not?"

"Well," Colette said thoughtfully, "Would you fancy an encounter with Gisele if you were a man?" And both of us fell about laughing again I am ashamed to say. But we were young then and knew very little about the cruelty of the world.

Aunt Titi, coming in with a large bowl of late roses, clicked her tongue. "Such frivolity! See that you get your work done!" Colette rolled her eyes at me impishly and we set to work. Discovering my sister as my friend was a new experience for me. I liked it.

*　　*　　*

"I have missed our walks in the evening, Etienne," I said boldly as I served him his soup. Etienne looked up in surprise. I didn't usually serve him. Nor did I make conversation as I served. But desperate circumstances require desperate measures, I decided. I had thought long and hard about Etienne, and I did not want him to drift away. I would do everything I could to make him aware that he was special to me. At once he asked me to walk later that evening and soon we were strolling toward the arena.

"And how are your mother and your two brothers in Nimes?" I asked as we walked, arm in arm.

"Very well, thanks. I plan to go home for a visit soon, early in Advent. Our work on the outside of the building is almost finished. We will start on the indoor work after a short break."

"Actually, I am going home to Saint Remy myself Sunday," I said. "To see my family before winter sets in."

"Ah yes, Saint Remy. I still have not been there." He smiled, recalling our earlier talk.

"You could come for a visit with me on the Sunday if you wished," I said boldly, looking at him through my lashes. "We wouldn't have room to put you up for the night, but you would be welcome to have the midday dinner with us," I offered, feeling as brazen as a hussy, the kind Aunt was always going on about. I was glad neither she nor Colette was in earshot.

"Why thank you, Minette, I would be delighted to accompany you. I could take the train back to Arles later in the day." And as we walked, I thought of Etienne and how much I admired him. Certainly he was more suitable for me than Vincent could ever be. My practical peasant mind grasped this certainty. I would not be swept toward disaster by an uncontrollable, unsuitable passion. No, always I would choose the steady, certain path. It was how I was made.

As autumn came to the Midi, days grew shorter, darkness dropped down suddenly as the shadows of the Alpilles lengthened. I was learning a lot about the colors of nature, reading the book on Millet Vincent had loaned me, but I had not seen Vincent for some time. I knew he must be in a frenzy trying to catch the fleeting sunshine of autumn. Now that he was living in the Little Yellow House, he made himself meals of a sort at home, to save money, so he did not come to the cafe often. But I doubted he was eating properly.

The last time I saw Vincent he said my portrait was finished, drying on the easel in the spare room of the loft. He promised to make a copy of it for me. I wanted very much to see it, but at the same time, I kept my thoughts distanced from Vincent as I grew certain that Etienne and I had the chance of a future together.

*   *   *

Etienne and I set out early Sunday for Saint Remy in the farmer's wagon, loaded down with butter, a ham, some jars of *confiture* of cherries, all gifts from Aunt Titi. Etienne brought wine from his mother's vineyard in Nimes, in an enormous raffia-covered jug. I had boxes of sugared almonds sent by Colette for Francine and my brothers. I had a big cake from the *patisserie* and a sack of coffee beans. We would all have a fine meal in honor of Etienne's visit. My mother, of course, knew he would be coming and that he was a possible suitor. I had written to her.

I reasoned with myself that if the shock of our humble

circumstances did not drive Etienne away, he and I might well become betrothed. We talked of our families as the wagon jolted along, and I discovered my admiration grew for Etienne's quiet, calm strength. He was a man of whom I could be proud. He shared with me his dream of owning his own land someday as we journeyed toward Saint Remy.

Saint Remy was at its most beautiful. The old plane trees had changed into giant golden yellow chalices full of dancing leaves. That made up for the somber, ordinary houses lining the way. The first glimpse of the slant-roofed house at the end brought a lump to my throat, creating in me a longing for that earlier, carefree time of childhood. But part of me wanted to move ahead, to discover the great mysteries of life, sampling its joys and its sorrows. Would it be my fate to live that life with the handsome, strong man seated beside me on the wagon?

My mother had dressed in her best black and looked quite distinguished as she greeted us. I was proud of her. Her father had been a schoolmaster who cruelly turned his back on her when she married beneath herself, married a farmer who owned no land, only rented it. So my mother never spoke of her family, but her love of books, her sense of self-worth, her strength of character in time of hardship all did her credit. They were the legacies from her estranged mother and father as surely as family jewels were passed from generation to generation. The gray eyes, the slender build, all came down to me through her, from those cold, distant grandparents whom I never knew.

At once Etienne endeared himself to my mother with his beautiful courtesy and the gift of the wine. He was quick to win over my brothers by asking them questions about the crops. A farmer's son himself, he knew the right questions to ask. We were a jolly company gathered for the meal around the old round table, groaning with the weight of good food. Francine shyly found her place beside me, stealing glances at Etienne through her long lashes. He captured her heart by playing cat's cradle with her and by making a white rabbit out of her napkin.

When we finally rose from the table, there was time only for a brief visit to the fields with my brothers, then it was time for him to return to Arles. As I stood beside the track watching the train carrying him farther away, the thought came to me, "I care for him more than I realize," and I began wishing I could be on my way back to Arles.

*   *   *

Colette and I were walking to Place Lamartine to receive the copy of my portrait Vincent had promised me. He could have brought it to the cafe, he said, but he wanted us to see a painting of his bedroom which he believed to be one of his best yet.

When I looked at the painting on the easel in the studio, I was struck by the disparity of the painting and the real room upstairs. The furnishings were the same, except for the addition of pictures above the bed. The change had come about solely through color. I was amazed. Vincent had deployed color boldly with great verve.

"Here I have used color in great harmony and simplification," he explained as we looked. "It is to be suggestive of rest, of sleep in general."

Colette's face took on a look of skepticism and Vincent hurried to explain further.

"The walls are pale violet. The floor is of red tiles. The wood of the bed and chairs is the yellow of fresh butter, the sheets and pillow cases a very light lemon-green. The coverlet is scarlet, the window green, the toilet table orange, the basin blue, the door is lilac, and that is all. There is nothing else in this room with its closed shutters. The broad lines of the furniture must again express inviolate rest. Portraits on the wall and a mirror and a towel and some clothes. That is all. The frame—since there is no white in the picture—will be white." He stood back, silent, waiting for our comments.

"It is lively, Vincent," I said quickly, "One of the most powerful paintings you have yet done. I like the absence of shadows. I like the flat colors." He smiled broadly, running his hands through the untidy shock of reddish blond hair.

"The flatness is taken from the style of Japanese prints. It is a contrast with the Night Cafe I painted which caused so much unhappiness for dear Madame Ginoux!" He smiled mischievously, the blue eyes darting first to me, then to Colette.

"I shall work at it again all day tomorrow, but you see how simple the concept is. I shall begin in the cool morning light so as to finish my canvas."

"Very nice, Monsieur Van Gogh," said Colette. She was courteous, but unenthusiastic. She did not like Vincent and he could sense her disapproval.

"And Mademoiselle Colette, are you enjoying your removal to Arles?" he inquired politely.

"Yes indeed, but of course my duties at the cafe have not permitted much time to explore the city yet." Colette's answer was rigidly polite. These two are at a stalemate, I thought.

"Where is the copy of my portrait, Vincent?" I said quickly.

He sorted through a group of framed pictures stacked against the studio wall. "Here it is. I have hung the original in my bedroom," he added, bringing a blush to my cheeks.

"Why Minette! It is you! The coloring is perfect." Colette gasped when she looked at the portrait.

"I call it Girl with the Coffee-Tinted Skin," Vincent said proudly.

"But the pink of the dress, the green of the background. It is perfection!" Clearly Colette was taken with the picture. Her eyes devoured it greedily.

I could see Vincent was enormously pleased. Nothing under heaven could persuade him to alter an image or a concept he believed in. To have his creation praised so extravagantly was heady stuff indeed. The portrait was framed in simple brown wood. I thought it was the most beautiful thing I had ever seen!

"Vincent, we must leave you. Aunt will expect us to be setting up the tables for lunch now. Thank you so very much for painting my portrait. I shall treasure it always."

"As will I, Minette," he answered softly, looking steadily at me as he handed it over. "Perhaps we will think of each other as we look at it?" he said so softly, I did not know whether or not Colette had heard. Already Vincent sounded in a strange way as though we were embarking on separate journeys. Or was I imagining it?

"I am almost finished with the Millet book," I said. "May I keep it a few days longer?"

"Certainly. I shall be coming to the cafe for a real meal before long as I weary of my feeble attempts at cooking. I will collect it then."

*   *   *

As for "The Girl with the Coffee-Tinted Skin", Aunt thought it was as beautiful as Colette did, and she wanted to hang it in the cafe, beside her portrait by Vincent. But I begged her to let me take it upstairs to my room, claiming I was too shy to let it be seen on public display.

"Thank goodness you brought it up here," Colette whispered as we took it upstairs. "Etienne wouldn't like it at all if you had it down in the cafe for everyone to see. And the old talk about you and Vincent would just start bubbling up again!"

CHAPTER ELEVEN

Most of the diners had left. It was after nine o'clock. Edith, who had begun working again in the evenings until my aunt could find a replacement for Gisele, was just leaving with her husband Charles when Vincent came in with the stranger. He was tall like Vincent with a powerfully-built figure. A peaky eagle nose, the faraway eyes of a sailor, long, straight black hair, his face mask-like, his expression dour. But there was a vitality about him I could not ignore. I sensed that he exuded tremendous energy in everything he did. I imagined that he was a man with a massive ego. I could almost feel the man's sensual presence.

Vincent went straight to my aunt, introducing Gauguin to her with a flourish. "My friend and fellow artist, Monsieur Paul Gauguin, my comrade, newly arrived from Brittany." Vincent was as proud as a puppy presenting a big bone.

Gauguin bowed over her hand, and with considerable charm said, "Madame. I am delighted. What joy it would give me to paint your portrait."

"Ah, for once I have the jump on you, old friend." Vincent quickly spoke up. "I have already painted Madame Ginoux." Vincent smiled broadly.

"Indeed?" Gauguin replied coldly. What tension there was

already between them, I thought. I could feel it, even standing some distance away. I remember the night was quite cold, for late October. I remember that there was a general sizing up of Gauguin by the patrons of the cafe who had never really welcomed Vincent with open arms. There were furtive glances, raised eyebrows, loud blowing of noses, the scraping of chairs. They guessed this man would prove to be every bit as odd as Vincent. This is what they were thinking, I imagined.

There was a quality of restless impatience in Gauguin as he spooned the stew Aunt Titi had brought to their table. A longing to be on his way, I thought. And Vincent, sensing this, hurried to oblige him. There was no doubt about who the dominant figure of that pair would be. Gauguin treated Vincent in an offhand way, almost like a servant. At least, that is how it seemed to me. And it made my blood boil.

It was obvious to me that in Vincent's mind Gauguin was master and teacher. Unquestioning, Vincent accorded to Gauguin the role of superior. He assumed the role of eager student, longing to please. This was the basis of the relationship from the beginning, as far as I could tell.

They did not tarry long that first night. In spite of urgings by my aunt to stay, they departed hastily. As Colette and I climbed the stairs for bed, the arrival of the strange man, Gauguin, in Arles was uppermost in our minds.

"Well, what did you think of him?" I said.

"Impossible!" she answered shortly. "Who does he think he is? Some potentate from the Far East in the disguise of a Breton fisherman?" She snorted. "And he's already made a pass at me, with his eyes."

"Colette!" I was shocked. He was old enough to be her father! Maybe even her grandfather! "What do you mean?"

"It was when I removed their plates," she said. "His eyes raked over my front, as though he was undressing me. Then he locked his eyes with mine in the most insolent way. Disgusting!" She gave a shiver.

I was silent for a minute, shocked that Gauguin would behave so. We were introduced to him as "Madame's nieces" by Vincent. Surely he had not misheard? "You are an *enfant* Minette." Colette laughed at my outraged expression. "Completely untouched by the ways of the world." I blushed. She had no right to tease me. But she spoke the truth. I knew I looked at the world through rose-colored spectacles. Had not my aunt told me over and over? My sister was much more of a realist than I.

"I know where they were going, why Gauguin was in so much of a rush," Colette said, her voice matter-of-fact. Of course I had to ask where.

"To the brothel," she answered. "I heard him telling Vincent to hurry, or the plumpest of the little chickens would already have been caught!"

"The nerve of him!" I raged. "And with a wife and all those children! He is a terrible influence on Vincent." My indignation knew no bounds. His poor, abandoned wife in Copenhagen, with all those children to feed. But my main concern was Vincent. I feared for him, feared the presence of this selfish, evil man whose vices and whose dominance might destroy Vincent. And I also had bossy words for my sister who was calmly preparing for bed.

"You watch out for him, Colette! Stay out of his way. He can only bring disaster wherever he goes."

"Never fear, Minette. I know what is on his mind. And he will get no cooperation from me."

And as we blew out our candle and settled in our beds in the darkened room, I heard the lonely hooting of an owl. Where on earth had it come from, I wondered. A stranger like Gauguin I thought, before dropping off to sleep.

*   *   *

The next time I saw Gauguin was at the market, where Aunt and I had gone early to get meat and vegetables for the cafe. A tinker had parked his caravan and mule at the edge of the market and had hung his supply of new, shiny pots and pans on the sides of the wagon, selling whatever he could. It was here we came upon Gauguin, carefully examining one of the larger pots and a frying pan.

"Ah, Monsieur Gauguin!" Aunt Titi's clarion voice rang out over the market hubbub. "You are looking for kitchen equipment? May we take it that you who create food for the soul in your paintings also create food for the stomach?"

Gauguin bowed toward us with the briefest of smiles. "Hardly, Madame," he answered in a condescending way. "I find our kitchen miserably lacking in equipment. Upon me falls the burden of preparing our daily fare, for Vincent can turn the kitchen into what resembles a war zone in a matter of seconds, with nothing palatable to show for it. I am forced by necessity to act."

As my aunt clucked sympathetically I thought, you are a guest in his house and yet you demean him. You will get no sympathy from me, you disloyal man. Gauguin, sensing my dislike, ignored me.

"And are your paintings going well, Monsieur?" my aunt asked politely. "I have been hoping you would ask me to paint my portrait."

"Well enough, Madame Ginoux," he bowed stiffly and turned abruptly away from us, gazing at the tinker's wares.

"Aunt," I whispered, "He does not paint with models. He paints from his imagination, not as Vincent paints."

Unconvinced and disappointed, she turned her attention to the marketing, still smarting from his snub.

*   *   *

Etienne and I had been walking out in the evenings several times a week. Although he was not at the cafe the night Vincent brought Gauguin, he was bound to have learned of his arrival from some of the other joiners who worked with him. Of course I knew

Etienne was aware of my special friendship with Vincent, even though I'd never had the opportunity to introduce them to each other.

However, he said nothing about Vincent to me, even when I showed him my portrait Vincent had painted. Although he admired it, still he said nothing. This reticence was a part of his personality. He was slow to act and certain of himself before he did. That is why I was surprised when on our evening stroll he suddenly said, "Minette, that painter friend of yours, Van Gogh, is in danger." Quickly I turned to him.

"What do you mean?" I was aware of a tightness in my throat as I struggled to appear nonchalant.

"His artist friend, Gauguin, is leading him into bad habits. He is drinking too much and he appears not to handle drink very well. Last night there was a fight between them at a bar. It could have become quite ugly. Some fellows managed to separate them and helped Van Gogh home and into his bed. He looked very ill."

Sick at heart to learn of the incident, I suddenly realized Etienne had been one of those who helped Vincent home. How else would he have known the details? So I put the question to him.

"Yes," he answered, saying nothing else. I knew I had to speak. His holding back must be because I had not clarified my thoughts toward him. He needed to know where I stood.

"Etienne, at one time I did have strong feelings for Vincent. But we were not suited for each other in so many ways. Still, I feel a tremendous sympathy for him. He has suffered so many disappointments and rejections in his life. But now he is only a friend. I do not care for him in any other way, not as you might suppose.

"He has loaned me his books, tried to instruct me a little about his work, created in me a wish to learn more. I am grateful to him for all that, and for painting my portrait. I wouldn't want tragedy to befall him."

"He is on a collision course with tragedy," Etienne said softly, "if he does not separate himself from Gauguin." Fingers of icy fear clutched at my heart.

"Etienne, why are you telling me these things?"

"Because I thought you might help him by talking to him, as a friend I mean."

I looked at him and spoke carefully. "I can talk to him in no other way, Etienne," I said softly. "My deepest feelings are for someone else. I think you know who that is."

And there on the pointed, painful cobbled streets Arles was infamous for, he gathered me carefully in his arms and kissed me, murmuring *ma petite, ma petite* over and over as he stroked my hair.

"All is well, now," he said, gently releasing me as we continued our walk. "Now we can decide when you will come to Nimes with me to meet my mother and brothers."

That night, before dropping off to sleep, I asked myself some difficult questions. Was I truly in love with Etienne? Did I still love Vincent? Would I be happy taking Etienne as a husband? And finally, was there any way I could lend a helping hand to Vincent?

*   *   *

At the wash house, the boring details of children's colds, the inferior quality of the butcher's meat, the price of eggs floated around me as I pounded the linens. The oppressive talk forced me to step outside for a breath of air.

"Minette! You refresh like a cup of cold spring water!" I spun around at the sound of that familiar voice. Vincent!

"You have not been to the cafe in ages," I complained to him as we faced each other outside the wash house.

"Ah, yes," he smiled ruefully. "It is Gauguin you see. The chap thinks he can cook. He is always stirring up some foul concoction for us to eat!" I smiled to myself, thinking of how Gauguin had expressed the identical view of Vincent's cooking when Aunt and I met him at the market. What conflicts must be seeping through the Little Yellow House! But I did not voice these thoughts. Instead I asked Vincent what he was working on.

"So much my head is spinning, Minette. You remember the four paintings of the Poet's Garden that I did?" I nodded. "Now Gauguin is working on a garden painting from memory with you and your aunt as the two women in the foreground. I must tell you he has put a large green bush beside you, a bush with a face!" How perfectly horrible, I thought, but in all honesty, nothing Gauguin did could ever be right as far as I was concerned.

"I am painting from memory now, Minette," Vincent said proudly. "A garden scene from Etten, where I lived as a child with my parents. Also, I am painting another portrait of you, from memory."

I was somewhat shocked that Gauguin had put me and Aunt Titi into his picture without a word to us. But then, it was only his imagination. I supposed I could be someone quite different, if he chose to see me that way. But I was pleased about Vincent painting me again.

"Tell me of the painting you are doing of me," I said.

"I call it the Novel Reader," he said. "It is a study of black and yellow, with you dressed in black, your hair piled on top of your head as you read a book. The background is chrome yellow, the walls of the room where you are sitting. By the way, are you still reading books?"

"Yes, Vincent, and I will always be grateful to you for encouraging me to broaden my horizons. I don't have much time, you know. But now I am reading one of Zola's novels."

"That is splendid, Minette. Nobody writes of the modern world better than Zola. You are my greatest success as a disciple!"

Secretly I studied the man standing before me. Did I imagine, or was there a heightened sense of stress? He was like a finely tuned violin, taut, waiting, expectant. His eyes gleamed almost as though he had a fever. His cheeks were redder than usual.

"And Monsieur Gauguin," I asked. "How is he?"

"Gauguin is still trying to adjust to the different climate of Provence. He has had great trouble with his digestion. Both of us have been ill, as a matter of fact. But we improve. As for Gauguin, he is still working like a dynamo, trying to teach me all that he knows. He has pointed out the many obvious errors in my work. He says all will improve in my style when I turn from painting before the subject to painting from memory."

Here he paused and looked searchingly at me. "Sometimes I am confused, Minette. I simply do not know how it is best for me to paint."

I wanted to cry out to him that he should be true to his own feelings and not be bound to anything Gauguin or anyone else tried to impose. But I dared not. Instead I said, "And the Novel Reader that is my portrait from memory? Are you pleased with how it is going?"

"Ah, that is the rub of it. I am not pleased. To me it is pallid and lifeless compared to the Girl with Coffee-Tinted Skin."

We stood there silently a few seconds and I summoned my courage. "Vincent, shouldn't you follow your own instincts? The sunflowers, your bedroom, Aunt Titi's portrait, all are so beautiful, and they are your unique emotional response to what you saw before you. So vital, so real. Maybe following your visual sensations is the best way for you to express your art."

I wanted to say more, wanted to urge him to stand up to Gauguin, tell him he was just as great a painter, probably greater. But I dared not. I was no painter. What did I know about it? But I could not restrain myself from blurting out, "You painted better before Gauguin came! Why can't you paint alone again, on your own?"

In his eyes I saw a sudden stab of fear and I realized Vincent could not face the world alone anymore. He needed someone, anyone, and Gauguin was all he had. Inwardly I wept at his dilemma. There was nothing more to be said.

*   *   *

I looked in the small mirror as I prepared for bed. My hair shone in the candlelight, the almond skin held a rosy glow. I opened the gray eyes wider. Having Vincent paint my portrait made me look at myself in a different way. Not a bad face at all, I thought brazenly. Etienne certainly seemed to like it. Since that kiss, we had grown closer to each other. There were no more sightings of Etienne walking with the baker's helper.

So why, I asked myself, did I continue thinking so much of Vincent? I could not get his predicament out of my mind. And it was really not my business whether Gauguin stayed or went. But it mattered to me greatly that Vincent was in peril. I believed with all my heart that Gauguin was an evil influence and would destroy Vincent if he remained in Arles. In spite of his large physical presence, Vincent inside was an innocent who believed the best in everyone and ignored the worst. He was delicate, even fragile inside.

Then I thought of Etienne, a true Provencal, strong, kind, a man whose roots were similar to mine. He is a man who too feels deeply, I thought, remembering that kiss we shared. But one who does not display emotions too quickly. I liked him all the better for it.

CHAPTER TWELVE

"I'm going out tonight," Colette said to me as we were finishing work for the day, removing dirty linen from the tables, saving the cloths which were clean for the next day.

"Oh?" I said absently, thinking again about Vincent and his problems. If only he would listen to me! I hurried to finish then went upstairs to brush my hair before Etienne arrived. When I returned, Colette had left. Etienne, Hubert and Edmond were waiting.

"Isn't Colette upstairs?" asked Edmond. "We thought she was with you."

"No, she just said she was going out. She didn't say with whom." Aunt Titi, appearing from the kitchen, could shed no light on the puzzle.

"Oh, well," I said with a laugh, "Colette has a mind of her own! We'll soon find her." But inside I was worried. Colette was not impetuous. On the contrary, she was level-headed and practical, much like our father had been. She had common sense beyond her years. For her to disappear like this was not like her at all.

At midnight I reluctantly locked the doors as Aunt Titi always insisted. Etienne too had worried, when we had not seen her all evening, but I told him I was sure she was upstairs in bed and sent him on his way after a lingering kiss. I did not want him to worry, but entering the darkened room, I knew at once she was not there.

Where could she have gone? The evening promenades around Arles were not lengthy. If she had been among those strolling, I knew I would have seen her. Sick with worry now, I dared not wake my aunt. Minutes crept by as I strained my ears to hear every sound. I imagined awful tragedies. Colette falling into the Rhone, Colette breaking a leg or an ankle clambering about the arena, or being chased by a band of ruffians. Colette alone, and needing me. It was horrible. The wind had come up and was rattling the window panes. I shivered. What should I do? I prayed for the sound of Colette's boots on the wickedly-pointed cobbles in the street below. Nothing. Only the phantom-like shadows cast on the walls of the room by my flickering, sputtering candle.

I must have dozed off, for I awoke hearing the clock in the church tower nearby strike two. Then I heard approaching footsteps outside my window. I flew downstairs after seeing the shape of two figures outside at the door. I opened the door as quietly as I could. Colette stood before me beside a man . . . . it was Vincent.

All sorts of thoughts exploded in my head, but knowing that she was safe made me embrace her without words and lead her inside. Anger, jealousy, betrayal, all those emotions clamored inside me, but one thought was paramount—my sister was safe! The door closed with a slight creaking sound and Vincent spoke softly, almost whispering.

"Your sister has had a great shock." His voice was grave, his words sad. "She needs all your care and concern." At once I put aside all thoughts of an assignation between Colette and Vincent. *He must have rescued her!* Vincent left after making sure that I would take charge. I quickly rebolted the door and we made our way upstairs on tiptoe. Colette had yet to say one word.

Safely in our room, Colette slipped out of her cloak and tears began to flow down her cheeks. There was an ugly rent in the front of the bodice of her dress, her arms were covered in bracelets of ugly red bruises and her face covered in tiny red blotches and scratches.

"Colette! What has happened to you? You look like you have been running in a meadow full of brambles, chased by a wild bull. You look like you have been assaulted!"

"You could say that," she replied, sobs choking her words. "In a way, that is what happened."

"Tell me," I ordered, gently leading her to a chair and beginning to bathe her poor face and wrists with cool water.

"He has been pestering me to walk in the evenings. I know I said to you I thought he was disgusting, but, well, I was attracted to him at the same time. The fact that he was so much older made me seem important, being able to interest an older man. I know you find this horrible, Minette, you are wincing at my words, but that is how it was. His appeal was both blatant and raw, no refinement at all. But women make such fools of themselves over men, don't they? I have made a fool of myself over Gauguin." Here she paused, and I could hardly believe it was my sister speaking. How had she become so worldly wise in such a short time? It defied explanation! And over Gauguin!

As if in a stupor, I stared at Colette's bruised wrists, remembering how she had disparaged Gauguin, called him a wife-deserter and a sponger. I could not believe my ears. "Go on," I said.

"It seemed harmless enough, I persuaded myself, a stroll around Arles. The streets would be full of people. I would avoid dark alleys. If we didn't go to the arena, we would go to the cloisters of Saint Trophime. I had it all planned. But it didn't work out that way. Instead, before I knew what was happening, he had brought me to the Alyscamps."

The Alyscamps! What a lonely, deserted, out of the way place to go, I thought. Not suitable at all for night strolling. Why it was outside the city walls.

"Yes," Colette resumed her account, "that is where we went. Nobody else was around. Of course, that was just what he had in mind. I was frightened, but I didn't want him to know it. There were a few innocent kisses, then before I realized what was happening he began grinding his mustache into my face and groping with the buttons of my dress, trying to unfasten the neck. Finally in an impatient rage, he simply ripped it open and began to fondle me. I was angry as well as frightened, but when I tried to beat him off, he just laughed and caught my wrists with one hand.

"We were still struggling, nothing had happened, when he simply bent over me and we both went down on the ground. I panicked then. I knew then he was intent on seducing me whether I was willing or not. His strength was such that I knew I could not stop him. He had a crazy look in his eyes." She stopped talking, looked down at her torn dress, the bruised wrists. She shook her head. She appeared dazed.

"Then what happened?" I said.

"Nothing. Everything. Some drunken seamen, probably from Saintes-Maries-sur-Mer lurched by, obviously having a night on the town. I screamed and screamed at the top of my voice and they started walking over to the bushes where we were. Gauguin dived farther into the bushes and I took off on a run for my life. I was running as fast as I could to get back within the walls. I did not want to run toward the cafe, I was afraid Gauguin would easily overtake me and go after me again. I had the idea to run to the gardens on Place Lamartine. I could watch the Little Yellow House and when he came home and went inside, then I knew I could run safely to the cafe."

"And is that what happened?"

"No. I saw a light when I got to the gardens, a light across the way, in the Little Yellow House. I knew Vincent was there, and that he would see me safely home. So I knocked on the door."

"And what did you tell him?"

"I told him the truth," she said simply. "And all the while I was talking to him, he had the saddest look on his face. To me he had the look of a prisoner who hears he is a condemned man. Why would it affect him that way? I'll never forget that look!"

I said nothing, but I knew Vincent was realizing the visit of Gauguin was indeed a disaster of cosmic proportions. Gauguin was in big trouble now. Visiting the brothels was one thing. Assaulting the fifteen year old niece of one of the town's respected citizens was something else again.

I bathed Colette's wrists and face as best I could and helped her get ready for bed. Other bruises were now visible on her upper arms and bosom, but thankfully, the high neck and long sleeves of her yellow dress would hide them. A heavy dusting of powder in the morning was all I could think of at present for her red, raw face.

"What will we do about Aunt Titi?" Colette asked, her eyes large. "She will know something is wrong. I, I don't want to go back home, Minette. I liked living here, until this happened." She turned her large eyes to me and again, the tears overflowed. Poor child, she had been through so much with that animal. Poor, foolish child.

"Don't fret, *ma petite,* we will think of something in the morning. Let's wait and see how your bruises look. Perhaps the best thing will be to say nothing at all . . . unless we have to. I'll mend your dress while you sleep and wash it in the morning. You can wear the yellow one tomorrow. It will cover your arms well. Everything will be all right, you'll see. Certainly Gauguin will keep quiet, and who else is to know?"

I spoke with a confidence I hardly felt. I wasn't worried about Gauguin. He would keep quiet to hide his outrageous behavior. Just thinking about it made me seethe with rage. But my concern was Vincent. His sense of justice and fairness might impel him to go to my aunt quickly, to inform her of the irresponsible behavior of one under his own roof at the expense of her young and innocent niece. I could almost hear his words! I resolved then in the dead of night as I looked at Colette that I would stop him from doing this at all costs. I must stop him, for Colette's sake!

Vincent's support of the underdog, the weak, was a part of his character. I remembered he had told me about taking in the sick prostitute Sien and her child. I recalled his overzealous ministrations to the poor people of the Borinage district in Belgium. Yes, I was sure I would have to convince Vincent that in this instance justice would best be served by silence.

As I tucked Colette between the covers, I smoothed her hair and she murmured, "Minette, you are so good to me. I have been such a fool, causing you so much worry. I am sorry."

"Hush, Colette. The main thing is you are all right. Your bruises will heal and this will all be forgotten. It could have been so much worse! Go to sleep, now." What a hard lesson for her to learn about taking risks, I thought. She looked so young and vulnerable lying there, not the self-possessed sister of old. Just a frightened, hurting adolescent.

I was reminded of the risk I'd taken not so many weeks earlier, going alone to see Vincent in the Little Yellow House. But for his sense of propriety, I might have done something I'd later have deeply regretted. Life is strange. We never know where it will take us.

I began the job of mending the dress, taking a strip out of the skirt so I could cut a new panel for the bodice. I used the torn part for underfacing. I worked until almost dawn, silently thanking my mother who had persevered, teaching me to sew when I was barely six. Those lessons saved the day. When I finished, the dress looked presentable. After it had been washed and pressed, it would look even better, the grass stains would disappear.

I let Colette sleep as long as I could without arousing Aunt's suspicions. Her face was much improved. The redness had almost disappeared, she looked quite normal. Dressed in her clothes, only a meticulous inspection would reveal anything out of the ordinary. Thank goodness the scratches had not broken the skin. As for Colette's mental state, she appeared calm and in control.

Vincent was another matter however. As I'd expected, he appeared right after breakfast. Fortunately Aunt Titi had left for the baker's to pick up the *baguettes*. Colette was laying places for the noonday meal. Quickly I intercepted Vincent and guided him through the kitchen into the backyard. We sat on a small bench where in the afternoon Monsieur Raspail smoked his foul-smelling pipes and read the daily newspaper. He was inside the kitchen now, busily preparing a *ragout* for lunch.

"How is Colette?" Vincent asked anxiously. His eyes held a worried look.

"She is fine," I said. "Relieved that she got away in time, feeling foolish that it happened. She slept well. Her bruises are much improved. She is wearing long sleeves and a high necked dress. Most of all, she now wants to put the episode behind her." I paused briefly for emphasis. "She greatly fears Aunt will find out about it and send her back home. She is desperate that this does not happen."

Vincent's brows flew up. "But surely her aunt should be told. Gauguin was in the wrong, surely Madame Ginoux would not send . . ."

"Oh, but she would," I hastily interrupted him. "She would not let anyone, certainly not her niece, continue working in her cafe if her reputation became tarnished in any way. Or even if it didn't, and people began talking! You know how she is, Vincent. Remember how upset she was about Gisele?" I pleaded with my eyes. He stroked his chin slowly.

"Minette, you are right of course," he replied after a pause. "I am a fool. I didn't think. I felt telling her the facts would be the right thing to do. But I have agonized over this all night. Gauguin is such a sensitive person. I am sure he meant no harm to Colette. He does not realize how the world looks at these things! He is not accustomed to a woman beating off his advances. Normally they clamor for him! He cannot have realized Colette was so young. Poor Colette, poor child. How can I help her?" He shook his head in a bewildered way.

Quickly I seized my chance. "The best way you can help her is to forget it ever happened and to say nothing to my aunt. Colette wants to forget it—then let her!" It upset me that as usual Vincent had made excuses for Gauguin. I longed to set him straight once and for all, but not at this moment. The danger to Colette was too great to detour from my cause: I had to keep Vincent quiet. Oh how I would have loved to box Gauguin's ears, evil man!

"Minette," Vincent said suddenly, "I would like to paint Colette! Maybe I could show her that I feel somewhat responsible for her painful episode with Gauguin. You see, if he had not come to stay in the Little Yellow House, this would not have happened. Do you think she would sit for me?"

*   *   *

And that is how Vincent came to paint Mousme, a Japanese girl, the portrait of a young girl he called "a Provencal version of a Japanese girl" with Colette as the model. She looked beautiful. She wore a red and blue striped blouse and a skirt of red dots on a blue ground. The background was plain, and her beautiful eyes were somewhat slanted, an almond shape, giving her a faintly Oriental look. Her left hand lay in her lap, the right arm was placed on the chair arm and showed her delicate wrist to perfection. The long, tapering fingers of her hand curled around the curve of the chair. She wore a dark ribbon in the back of her hair which was parted in the middle and pulled tightly back. It was a delightful portrait of youth and innocence.

CHAPTER THIRTEEN

Of course after the shameful episode with Colette, Gauguin did not appear at the cafe, but I saw him from a distance frequently, swaggering about the town. He seemed to me to have lost a little of his insolence, his cocksure personality. In one way, Colette had won a small victory. She had escaped unscathed, with minimal physical hurts. Her inside thoughts were another matter. But it was good to see her laughing again as she went on her strolls with Edmond and Hubert, who had become as close as family to her. I believed Colette was trying to keep her life happy and uncomplicated until all the wounds to her heart were healed. We didn't talk anymore about it.

As the season of Advent and Noel approached, my thoughts turned to my family in Saint Remy. Aunt Titi had promised to close the cafe a few days after Noel so we could go home. But before we could make definite plans, Etienne invited me to spend a few days at his mother's home in Nimes.

Aunt Titi was enthusiastic and immediately engaged Edith to work in my absence. Edith was finding staying in their one room for days on end was boring, and she liked having a little money of her own. I gathered Charles only doled out for the necessities, and with the greatest reluctance. I wrote to my mother of the plan and she joyfully consented. She had given her unspoken approval to Etienne when she first met him, and now that the bountiful harvest was over, she faced the future with much more assurance.

An excitement filled me when I thought of making the trip with Etienne, then meeting his family. But there was also apprehension! What if I did not meet with the family's approval? What if somehow I fell short? I had no illusions—Etienne was taking me along for a purpose. If I passed muster, he would ask me to marry him. It was as simple as that.

If not, then he would probably stop seeing me and look for someone else. Etienne was a strong man, but he was practical too, and I did not believe he would defy his family.

Plans were made to go the Saturday before Christmas. We would stay overnight Saturday and Sunday, returning early Monday.

Vincent had begun coming to the cafe alone, explaining to Aunt Titi that Gauguin had a stomach complaint or that he was busy working on a painting and could not be persuaded to leave it. Colette and I of course knew the real reason. Gauguin did not want to face Colette. What a coward the man was! He must have realized I too knew of that horrible night at the Alyscamps, and didn't want to feel the lash of my sharp tongue!

Vincent had been working on a vineyard scene, "where the vines are turned red by the setting sun, like a sea of red wine." Dotted among the vines, harvesting the grapes, were the figures of the women, bending mushroom shapes in their dark purplish-blue skirts. A horse and cart stood waiting at the edge of the vineyard to take the grapes to the press along a road as yellow as paved gold, shimmering and iridescent, with the gigantic orb of the setting sun tinting everything it touched in the picture. I thought is was one of the most expressive works Vincent had ever painted, and I was quick to tell him so.

The size was thirty by thirty-six inches, and he called it The Red Vineyard. Many years later, I read somewhere that it was the only picture of his that ever sold during his lifetime. At this time he was also working on several versions of The Sower inspired by Millet, whose peasant studies Vincent idolized. The sower, with its Biblical associations, was a motif Vincent returned to over and over again.

He painted two Sower oils in December of that year, both oriental in feeling. Citron moons, or setting suns over dark, purple fields, with the black, solitary figure of the sower striding along the rows, in one the picture plane divided into a diagonal by a giant pollarded tree trunk leaning toward the yellow moon, slicing the picture into two triangles.

Vincent said the idea for the painting came to him one night on an evening walk, just as the Red Vineyard had done. I thought the coloring, a green and yellow sky and purple fields, was compelling.

Just as Gauguin had painted a garden scene as an answer to Vincent's series on the Poet's Garden, he also painted a scene of women of Arles washing, just as Vincent had done. Vincent painted women of Arles washing on three of the canals around the city. The municipal wash house, which I used, was much closer, but not nearly so picturesque as women washing in the open country with landscape as a background. "Nothing is so appealing as blanchesseuses washing in an open stream," he told me. The site he liked best was the washing station at the Roubine du Roi. The picture viewpoint was high, he looked down on the working women from the top of the embankment.

To my mind, Gauguin's painting lacked the sparkle and animation of Vincent's. Vincent brought them to the cafe one evening to show us, full of praise as always for Gauguin's achievements. Why did he always have to kowtow to Gauguin?

"And how are things with you and Gauguin?" I asked, when we had finished looking at the pictures.

"After many threats to me to leave, he has finally written to my brother in Paris to tell him that he cannot remain here with me, that we are quarreling all of the time." Here Vincent paused for some time, as though thinking of how to phrase his next words.

"I think Gauguin is being a little bit overdramatic. I think like most people we have our disagreements, but on the whole, we learn a lot about each other."

Always the optimist, Vincent, I thought. And how like Gauguin to threaten to leave! It was his ploy to gain the upper hand with Vincent. "And if he goes?" I asked.

"Then he goes. I am all calm and serenity. Whatever happens, happens." But I noticed his hands twisted nervously as he talked, and the look in his eyes was strange, somewhat unfocused. Had he been drinking again, I wondered?

Earlier, in the summer, he had confessed once to me that he was able to maintain the fever pitch of his summer achievements only because he subsisted on strong coffee and alcohol. He said it "kept me hitting the high yellow note" of all those wonderful summer pictures of flowers and harvests.

It is true, he had been in the fields every moment of daylight, which was considerable at summer's peak, leaving the Little Yellow House before sunrise, wearing the wide-brimmed straw hat, attacking canvas after canvas, day after day.

Now that the days were so short, he was forced to work in the studio, throwing the two of them together more and more. I knew Vincent suffered terribly from the cold. He told me once he had picked Arles because it was a haven of warmth and sunshine. True in the summer, of course, but on the February day when he arrived, there was a snowstorm!

What if he was keeping up his nervous energy, his incredible vision, with coffee and alcohol? I felt that coping with the eccentric, egotistic personality of Gauguin put a terrible strain on him, but the fear of loneliness prodded him onward. The situation was dangerous.

He had invested so much of himself in the Little Yellow House. It had become a symbol of a haven, stability, an oasis of peace in a clamoring world. Vincent would do anything to keep Theo supporting the "Studio of the South."

On that night, when Vincent came to the cafe, Etienne also

appeared, and for the first time I was able to introduce them properly.

"Why I remember you," Vincent said immediately. "You were one of the Good Samaritans who helped me home one night when I was a bit the worse for wear." He smiled apologetically.

"What a pleasure, Monsieur Van Gogh. Minette has shown me the portrait you painted of her. It is enchanting." Etienne made no reference to the unfortunate incident.

"Why thank you, Monsieur Martin. With such a beautiful subject as Minette, any artist could create a masterpiece! May I call you Etienne? I hope you will call me Vincent."

Embarrassed, I stood between them thinking, what are their true thoughts? But it was impossible to tell. I made a silent prayer: let them like each other.

"Since I arrived in Arles last February in a snow storm, Minette has been my dearest friend, and my most truthful critic!" Here Vincent stopped and looked fondly at me. Etienne smiled. They were getting on well enough, but I wished they would move to a subject other than me.

Vincent began to question Etienne about Nimes, asking him about the light, the vegetation, and the famous landmark of Nimes, the big aqueduct, the *Pont du Gard*. "I hope sometime to visit there," Vincent added. "I would also like to view the fine Roman temple, the *Maison Carre*."

He stopped talking and looked closely at Etienne. "I would like to paint you sometime Etienne. Would you sit for me?"

"It would be an honor," answered Etienne smiling. "I am at your disposal." Inside me, a knot was slowly dissolving in the region of my heart. They liked each other. It was going to be all right.

Arrangements were made that night to paint the portrait. Vincent was in a frenzy to begin. He suggested the next Sunday afternoon. Would Etienne come? And of course, Mademoiselle Minette would be welcome also.

"Perfect," I said. "I know Aunt can spare me Sunday afternoon." And so it was all arranged.

"Sunday afternoon it shall be!" Vincent answered. "Then I shall have portraits of two of my best friends during my Arles days."

At the time, I thought nothing of his reply. Thinking back over the years however, I have wondered over and over why those words had not alerted me as we sat together in the cafe talking. Was Vincent aware, in some intuitive way, that his time in Arles was coming to an end?

*   *   *

While Etienne was having his portrait painted, I was making preparations for Noel. I was making a warm jacket for Francine out of an old woolen cape Aunt Titi had given me. The jacket was tight fitting and waist length, with gay embroidered sunflowers running along the front closings and the hem. I knew she would love the brightness of the flowers. I was in the midst of knitting warm woolen caps for my brothers, and as a surprise for Colette, I was sewing a blouse of the softest white lawn.

I had found a lovely tortoise shell comb for my mother who, like Aunt Titi, was very proud of her hair. The comb was set with studs that gleamed silver in the light. For Aunt Titi I was embroidering a new apron, white embroidery on white linen. It would not be fussy, she could wear it at the cafe. But it would be of a beautiful quality.

For Etienne, I was hemstitching linen handkerchiefs. I decided to crochet a lace cap for his mother, as a sort of thank you present for inviting me to stay. The problem of Vincent was more difficult. In the end, I selected the latest novel by Emile Zola at the only bookshop in Arles. The owner, Monsieur Philipe, assured me that he had not sold a copy to Vincent.

*   *   *

Etienne's portrait, painted on a twenty-one by twenty-five inch canvas, was a striking likeness. Etienne, seated, looked directly at the viewer. He wore a mimosa yellow jacket and a jaunty snap-brim black hat. A white shirt and black vest showed slightly beneath the coat.

His skin tones were vital and alive, heightened by youth and good health, but Vincent concentrated on the remarkable green eyes and dark hair, making the strong features the focus of the entire painting. The eyes were luminous under finely detailed, sensitive brows. Candid, debonair, nonchalant—Vincent captured the essence of Etienne. I thought it was one of the best portraits ever painted by Vincent.

Vincent too seemed very pleased, calling it "The Young Frenchman of Modern Times." As for Etienne, he said little, but I knew he was pleased.

When we were in the Little Yellow House on Sunday afternoons for sittings, the house was strangely silent. Once Vincent mentioned that Gauguin was in bed with a stomach complaint. Another time he merely said Gauguin was out.

It was easy to see that they were avoiding each other. Apparently living together in the Little Yellow House had become something like an armed truce for them. Vincent on the one hand hoping against hope things would get better, the optimist's view; Gauguin, weary beyond words with the untidiness and chaos in which Vincent, unseeing, lived, yet fearful of losing Theo's support if he bolted. What a tinderbox! Once I heard the front door close as we were in the studio and the sound of footsteps going upstairs. But Vincent said nothing. I knew it had to be Gauguin.

As for my unchaperoned visits to the studio of the Little Yellow House in the presence of not one, but two men, you may well wonder! But my aunt saw Etienne as different. If we weren't officially betrothed, we soon would be, she reckoned, and she trusted his good judgment and common sense implicitly. And she liked him into the bargain. He had won her seal of approval.

CHAPTER FOURTEEN

At the final sitting for his portrait, Etienne told Vincent we were planning to leave Saturday for Nimes, to be with his family. We planned to return early Monday. Vincent expressed surprise, and delight.

"Ah, so you will be taking Minette to meet your family," he said.

"Well yes, my mother and two brothers. I wondered if perhaps you might like to come along with us? You said once you would like to see Nimes, and I could show you around with Minette. I've already written to my mother. She will make you welcome."

I turned quickly toward Vincent to catch his reaction to this surprise invitation. I wondered how Etienne's mother, whom I already dreaded meeting, would feel about an eccentric Dutchman who spoke with great intelligence yet whose appearance was strange, to say the least. But I knew Etienne would leave nothing to chance.

Vincent was touched. He looked at Etienne carefully before he spoke. "You would take me into your home, a rough, unpolished Dutchman? Etienne, I am deeply moved."

"It would be a chance for you to see another corner of Provence," Etienne shrugged. "It would be no trouble." In few words, Etienne had made the invitation seem the most natural thing in the world. I reminded myself of my good fortune in finding such a man.

"The problem is, it is a particularly difficult time for me at the moment," Vincent said thoughtfully, examining his brushes, his eyes downcast. "Gauguin who is staying here as you know, may be leaving quite soon. I do not know. But at any rate I cannot in good conscience leave him here alone. He is a stranger to Arles, and I am his host."

Humph, I thought. Gauguin already had a reputation in Arles for being selfish, rude and impossibly arrogant. He was no stranger to the people of Arles! Why did Vincent eternally show such unwavering loyalty to that ungrateful man! I would never understand it.

And so it was not going to happen. But Etienne realized along with me how pleased Vincent had been to receive the invitation. He said he would come by the cafe on the Monday night after we returned, to hear about our visit.

Etienne's heart was in the right place, I reflected. With a pang I realized it had never occurred to me to ask poor Vincent to go to my home in Saint Remy. I had been so self-absorbed, I hadn't given it a thought. My respect for Etienne soared.

*   *   *

On our way at last, Etienne pointed out places of interest along the route. We were traveling in a northeasterly direction. Surprisingly, the land was a warm silver gray, echoing the hundreds and thousands of olive trees covering every hillside. Great white rocks lurked among trees swaying gently in the breeze. Thank goodness the *mistral* winds were calm. Harvesting was just over, the olives gathered in and delivered to the presses. Etienne told me there were olive groves on his family's farm that had been growing for generations.

Our journey through the town of Nimes was hurried as we were anxious to arrive at the *mas*, or farm house of Etrienne's mother.

On a small road off the main road lined with olive trees on both sides we made our way. Then the carriage made a sharp turn between a double row of plane trees. I could see the *mas*. Two stories with a sloping one story addition, the walls were ocher color and the roof made of terra cotta tiles. Etienne told me the walls were stone, covered in stucco for a more attractive appearance. It was very old, more than a hundred years old, and built by a great, great grandfather Martin.

The house faced south with a slight turning to the east to avoid the direct blast of the *mistral* winds. Near the house on the north side in order to block the cold, a tightly planted row of cypresses stood sentinel, a windbreak. On the south, plane and lotus trees provided shade in summer.

The house had a somewhat austere appearance mainly because of the lack of windows. None at all on the north side, while on the south the windows were small, to keep out the burning summer sun and heat.

Overall, the *mas* was impressive. Certainly bigger and finer than my mother's house in Saint Remy. I blushed to think of how humble that place must have seemed to Etienne yet he appeared indifferent to the poor surroundings. Silently I raised my chin a little and straightened my back. I would not allow Etienne's *maman* to see me tired and drooping from the trip, slumping as we approached.

"Come, Minette!" Etienne sprang out and lifted his arms to me. He was smiling. As he helped me down he whispered in my ear, "Don't be put off if *maman* seems a bit abrupt. It is just her way. She means nothing." He gave my hand a squeeze.

As we entered through the heavy carved door, I became aware of dark wood cupboards and ornately decorated chests, an enormous fireplace, a large oval table surrounded by ladderback chairs with cushions in a small—figured red print. Madame Martin was at the huge black range in the kitchen, bending over a simmering pot.

"*Maman!*" Etienne hurried to embrace a tiny, birdlike woman in voluminous black skirts and encased in a stiffly starched white apron glistening with cleanliness. Her gray hair was parted in the middle and upswept and her eyes were brown wren eyes, alert and inquisitive. Her thin lips stretched into a smile. Her skin was ivory like old alabaster and very beautiful.

"Madame Martin," I said putting out my hand and bobbing as Etienne introduced me.

"You are welcome," she murmured without much warmth, I thought, then I chided myself for making early judgments. The brown marble eyes looked at me intently. "You are not the usual Arlesienne type with all that black hair, the large neck. But you have the nose."

Somehow I already felt I had not measured up. "I come from Saint Remy," I said. "I have lived in Arles only since February." As though that might explain the gray eyes, the ash colored hair.

"So Etienne has written me. Still, you have the dark skin of the Arlesienne." Turning to Etienne she added, "Take Mademoiselle Minette upstairs to the blue room next to mine. Etienne, you will stay at the *cabane* with Pierre." I knew Pierre was one of the older brothers, the one who was not married. But what was a *cabane*?

Etienne explained later the *cabane* was the small two-room house the farm manager, or *guardian* occupied so as to be near his beasts. It was curved with rounded walls like the apse of a church at the north end to protect it better from the wind. The roof was made of rushes.

"I'll take you to look at it later after you've rested a bit from the trip," he said.

And so I began to unpack in a small and cheerful room under the eaves with a high bed covered in blue gingham with matching curtains at the small windows. A red geranium bloomed on the sill. The walls were plain and whitewashed. A large old fruitwood cupboard covered in carvings of Biblical scenes stood opposite the bed. It looked very old but was beautifully polished. A ladderback chair and a washstand were the only other pieces of furniture in the room.

The room smelled sweetly of lavender and when I opened the cupboard, I found bags of lavender hanging inside. Other bags tied with small blue ribbons hung from the bed's posters. What a charming custom, I thought. Madame Martin was indeed a good housekeeper.

Unpacking was the work of a few moments. After washing my face and hands, I looked out the window, uncertain whether to go down so quickly or not. I saw Etienne embrace a tall, slightly older version of himself in the courtyard in front of the house. Pierre. How much alike they looked, except for wrinkles etched in the forehead of the older man from long hours working in the sun and wind.

The big family meal would take place this evening, giving Etienne plenty of time to show me the famous Roman aqueduct, the *Pont du Gard* and other Roman antiquities the next day. Summoning all my courage, I gathered up the two jars of brandied peaches sent by Aunt Titi as a gift and hurried downstairs. Madame Martin perched like a restless setting hen on the cushion of a straight back chair, eyes riveted on my approach. I noticed her back did not touch the chair, so erect was her spine.

"My aunt, Madame Ginoux, sends you these white peaches in brandy. They are a specialty of hers. She hopes you enjoy them."

"I do not take spirits," she said sharply, then noticing that my face fell, she said somewhat more softly, "It is kind and thoughtful of her to remember me. Of course I will try them and you may be sure, Etienne and the others will relish them. Please give Madame Ginoux my sincere thanks."

So that little bump in the road is past, I thought, offering to lay the table or do anything she might suggest.

"There is no need. All is prepared, the table is laid. Etienne will be here soon to take you for a quick stroll around before dark. The others will be arriving for dinner soon." Quickly I looked toward her table. There appeared to be ten places. Etienne and myself, Pierre and his mother, the other brother Paul and his wife—surely they did not have four children! But I said nothing.

*   *   *

Madame Martin had outdone herself by preparing a *bouillabaisse* for our dinner. We were all gathered around the table as Etienne brought in the steaming tureen. The unknown guests to whom I was readily introduced were the other brother Paul, his wife Marguerite and their son, little Paul. A neighboring family, mother, father and daughter Agnes, the Roussilons, made up the party.

Agnes Roussilon was beautiful, that was indisputable. She had a halo of brown curls and a dress of pink frills and ribbons billowing like some cloud an angel would rest on, I thought, somewhat waspishly. The neck of her gown was low cut to display an ample bosom and a fair skin. Her beauty was so delicate and dainty I felt at once transformed into something clumsy and awkward, who hardly deserved a place in her presence. I thought my dark skin must look coarse, compared to her milky whiteness.

I was wearing the rose print dress in which I had been painted by Vincent, but it no longer pleased me. It looked like a workaday dress beside the shiny pink and white striped sateen of Agnes's dress. As Madame Martin ladled out the rich *bouillabaisse* my spirits sank to the bottom of the tureen. I began to wonder why I had come. Then I was aware of Etienne's voice.

He was telling the company about how I had been painted by the artist from Paris living at present in Arles. He described the beauty of the portrait with great warmth and pointed out that I was wearing the dress in which I'd been painted. Suddenly Paul and Marguerite were asking questions. What was it like, sitting for a portrait? Did I grow tired? Could I speak? And so on. I was so busy answering their questions I forgot to worry about how I looked. Bless Etienne!

Agnes was clearly the apple of Madame Martin's eye and was allowed to assist in passing the toast with which we lined our bowls before the rich seafood and broth were ladled in. Loup, turbot, mussels, sole and crayfish were the ingredients of the dish, along with onion, garlic, tomato, broth and a liberal splashing of white wine.

Etienne kept refilling our glasses with the wine of his family's vineyard and soon the party became quite lively. Even Madame Martin allowed him to pour her a small glass of wine. Agnes, obviously a favorite with Etienne's family, was in an animated mood. She blushed becomingly as Paul teased her about her escort to the *santon* fair at Marseilles recently. I saw her gaze linger on Etienne, hoping he would notice her. But his arm rested comfortably on the back of my chair after we had finished eating.

She may have been a year or so older than Etienne, it was impossible to tell. His manner to her was friendly, but not in any way special, or possessive. I was grateful for that. Then I suddenly realized, that had been his attitude toward me for a long time, but we were closer now.

After everyone had finished the table was cleared and the *santon* figures were brought out. These small figures, "little saints," portraying the Nativity, appeared in Provence when the churches were closed during the revolution. Mary, Joseph, the Babe, the usual ox and ass were the principal figures, but as *santons* became more popular, other figures were added, wise men, angels, shepherds, then blacksmiths, milkmaids, huntsmen, farmers and so on.

The figures of Madame Martin's *santon* collection came from many sources and were of varying ages. Clearly some of the figures she must have had as a child. Others were probably acquired as her children were growing up.

Most were made of clay. There were a few carved in wood, beautifully and colorfully dressed. I had never seen such a collection. I knew Aunt Titi had a collection which would be set up on Christmas Eve, but I had not seen it yet. *Santon* fairs, such as the one Agnes recently attended in Marseilles, were held for the buying and selling of figures, although in rural areas, many families made their own in the long, dark winter evenings.

The Roussilons invited us all to visit their house the following day after mass. Madame Martin's face quickly broke into a smile, then Etienne spoke up quickly, thanking them warmly, but he said he had promised to take me to see the sights of Nimes, starting with the old church, where we would go to mass. Then the arena, the Baths of Diana, and finally the aqueduct. It was my first visit to the area, he explained.

"Another time, perhaps," Madame Roussilon replied, somewhat tight-lipped. She sees me as a threat to Agnes, whom she wants to marry Etienne, just as his *maman* wishes, I thought. After the visitors left, I bid everyone goodnight, then hastened up the stairs. The trip had been tiring, but it was as nothing compared with the undercurrents running through the evening with Agnes and her parents. Quickly I closed my door and leaned on it in relief. I went to the little window and opened the casement for a breath of fresh air.

Immediately the voices of Etienne and Madame Martin wafted up to me. I could not catch all the words, but I heard enough to discover it was an argument, about me. I heard her ask Etienne if he was decided on his course. Had he asked me yet to marry him? He answered that he had not, but that he planned to do so soon.

"Once and for all, *Maman*, I do not wish to marry Agnes and I never shall. I love Minette dearly." He bid her a courteous goodnight and vanished in the direction of the *cabane*.

So I was left to ponder the angry words of mother and son. I was happy at Etienne's declaration of love for me, proud of him for standing up to his mother, but I feared the wrath of his mother, if she decided she would oppose our marriage. Surely that would not happen. They were a family with more wealth than mine—as were the Roussilons—but our families were all farmers, we made our living from the land. Surely she would not try to maneuver Etienne's affections. I worried about it until I finally slept.

*   *   *

Etienne and I had little time to talk before we left. Breakfast was a quick meal with his mother and Pierre, then we were off. The carriage took us quickly into Nimes, to the cathedral of Notre

Dame and Saint Caster and we hurried inside as mass was just beginning. It was a very old cathedral, first built in 1096, Etienne told me, but recently it had been almost completely reconstructed. After mass we went directly to the *Maison Carre,* a perfectly designed Greek temple built by the Romans in the first century before Christ. Close by we explored the arena, which is in a better state of preservation than the one in Arles, although both hold about 21,000 people at the bull fights in the summer.

We went on to look at more Roman ruins. The Baths of Diana were deserted in the chill of December, and we clambered about the trees and bowers of the lovely gardens surrounding the ruins. Etienne told me the gardens were developed in the 18th century. We were sitting alone in the sunlight on an iron bench.

"You enjoyed the dinner last night?" he asked.

"Oh yes, and meeting the others in your family."

"And Agnes?"

I replied that she was very pretty. I did not add that she was skilled in showing herself to the best advantage, and adept at stealing all the attention.

Etienne spat out his words. "Such a show-off! And she is not nearly so pretty as you!" I looked at him in surprise and he threw up his hands.

"Frankly, I am a little sick of Agnes! Everyone has been trying to get us betrothed for years. If you must know, Minette, that is one reason why I decided to come to Arles and work as a joiner. I wanted to get away from Agnes!"

I stole a look at him. His fists were clenched, and two red spots burned in each cheek. Where was the cool, self-possessed Etienne I knew? "But your mother, she will be so disappointed if you do not . . ." Quickly he interrupted.

"If I don't marry her? She knows by now it will never happen. She will just have to get used to the idea that I want to marry someone else!" There seemed little I could say at this point. Silently I looked up at him. He looked like a student preparing to recite a difficult examination before the teacher.

"You mean so much to me, Minette," he began. "I find you have moved straight into my heart, whether by accident or not, I don't know. I only know I love you and want you to be my wife."

Still I said nothing. I could not believe that he preferred me to the glamorous Agnes, a bird of paradise compared to the plain brown sparrow sitting beside him. As if understanding my doubts, he gathered me in his arms and kissed me soundly. "You are my Diana, Minette," he whispered huskily in my ear.

Then I was able to tell him that I loved him with all my heart.

"Now we are betrothed," he smiled down at me. "Will you wear this brooch of my grandmother's as a token?" He took out of his pocket a small silver circle enameled with tiny flowers delicately painted in pink and blue.

"Etienne," I said, "it is lovely, but surely your mother . . ."

"Suggested I give it to you," he finished. "See, she is not an ogre as you might have imagined. I saw you at your window last night, Minette, and realized you had overhead everything. But you did not see my mother come to me with the brooch before breakfast and tell me her preference for Agnes was misplaced, that she thought you were a fine girl and she knew you would make me a good wife. She looks forward to becoming a mother to you." Then carefully he pinned the brooch to the collar of my dress.

"I talked to her this morning of my plans before you came downstairs. I will continue to work in Arles until we are ready to be married. Then, with the money I have saved, I will buy land to farm, and we will move here to live. I will have my own land, and hopefully there will be many children to help me farm it."

I blushed at his words, but I felt thrilled all the same. I would be the wife of a landowner, the son of a respected family. The joy of it brought tears to my eyes. And I had met with the approval of Etienne's *maman*.

Who can remember, or would want to share, all of the sweet words which gushed out between us as we sat in the ruins of the Baths of Diana? We could not linger long, as we had to travel twelve miles to the *Pont du Gard*, the famous old aqueduct constructed by the Romans. Perfect in proportion, it had been recently brought back to its original splendor by Napoleon III. As we stood looking at the old bridge I felt proud of my Provence, mine and Etienne's.

Supper that evening back at the *mas* was a simple affair, but Madame Martin let me assist her. She seemed much more accepting of me, and she smiled when she saw I was wearing the brooch. "It suits you," she said, and Etienne agreed. I was beginning to like her, and to relax in my surroundings. Madame Martin had proved herself a diplomat.

CHAPTER FIFTEEN

The mound of butter carefully wrapped in vine leaves, the wine, a dozen eggs from *Maman's* special hens, all were carefully packed into the carriage as we made our departure. But most importantly, I carried Madame Martin's quiet approval as I said goodbye. "Come back soon," she said unexpectedly. For the first time, I felt a natural response to her. I took her hand and pressed it.

Remembering Vincent's plan to come by the cafe in the evening, we decided to keep our betrothal a secret until then. Instead, I told Aunt Titi and Colette about the Martin *mas*, the antiquities of Nimes, the *Pont du Gard*. But by late Monday evening, Vincent still did not come! He had been so enthusiastic about our journey. Surely he did not forget. Etienne and I wondered at his failure to appear.

In the end, we told Aunt and Colette of our wedding plans and they were both delighted. But we decided to keep all a secret from everyone else until we sent a letter to my mother in Saint Remy.

*   *   *

The next morning I was cutting up the bread when I saw the

tall, lank figure of the Prefect approaching the cafe. My first thoughts were of Gisele. Could he possibly have brought news of her? His long sideburns matched his somber appearance, I thought, as I lowered my gaze and hurried to summon my aunt who was engaged in a heated argument with the cook, Monsieur Raspail, about the proper sauce to serve with the entrecote steak on the luncheon menu.

Aunt Titi brushed a stray strand of hair from her temple, adjusted her immaculate apron and hurried into the cafe. I tried to blend into the wallpaper as they spoke while I was cutting the bread at the serving table. I managed to hear every word.

"After a violent quarrel between Monsieur Van Gogh and his painter friend Paul Gauguin last night at the artist's residence on Place Lamartine," he began, and my heart froze, "Monsieur Gauguin left the house and went to a hotel where he booked a room for the night."

"*Mon Dieu,*" breathed Aunt Titi as the Prefect set his thin lips into a line and pressed his spectacles more firmly on his bulbous nose.

"Monsieur Van Gogh, who seemed to be out of his mind, at some point seized a kitchen knife at the house and cut off a part of his own ear. Later, at the *Maison de Tolerance Number One*, he gained entry, asked to see the girl named Gisele, handed over a bloody handkerchief containing his ear and saying, 'Keep this object carefully,' after which he departed abruptly to return to his house and went to bed."

"What horror!" breathed my aunt, her handkerchief to her mouth.

"He was discovered there by the police this very morning, hardly an hour ago, showing almost no sign of life. He has been taken to hospital now. The girl Gisele went into a fit of hysterics last night when she opened the handkerchief, and had to be sedated. They are interrogating her now as we speak. It appears there was no reason he chose her to receive the ah, handkerchief."

The bread knife I was holding suddenly swam before my eyes,

I felt my body swaying and heard my aunt's voice, "Catch her! She is falling!"

When I opened my eyes I was stretched out on the floor of the cafe. My aunt was fanning me vigorously with her apron and the Prefect was bending over me, peering down through the thick lens of his spectacles. Embarrassed, I tried to rise, but my aunt held me down.

"It is nothing more than a fainting spell, Monsieur. She will recover presently. The talk of the, ah, mutilation must have caused it. Poor child. These young girls are so delicate." With her assurances, he bowed stiffly, backed off and made his way to the door.

"Strange man," muttered my aunt after he had disappeared. "Do not fret, Minette. You will be fine in a moment. Lie there quietly and I will bring you water."

I drank the cool water and immediately began to feel more like myself. The lightheadedness disappeared. But Vincent in the hospital . . . after cutting off part of his ear! I felt sick at heart.

"What could have driven him to it, Aunt?" I whispered.

"I do not know, Minette. Poor sufferer. We must be strong and give him what help we can. Who knows what torments plague him?" As I looked at Aunt Titi I realized what a generous, loving heart she had. I was lucky to be in her care.

"I am wondering what treachery on the part of Gauguin drove him to this!" I said.

"Hush, hush, Minette. We must not make a judgment until we know the facts." And she sent me upstairs to rest for a bit. I was sleeping when Colette came to tell me it was time for lunch.

The cafe was buzzing like an angry swarm of bees with the news. Such a thing had never happened before in Arles some said. This was what you could expect of foreigners, part savages, whose ways are not like ours. "On the contrary," said still another voice. "He is mad. He does not know what he does." Eyes rolled heavenward. The babble ebbed and eddied around us as we served the food.

I handled my orders quietly, trying not to listen, but of course that was impossible. It took all of my will power to get through my work that noontime. Out of the corner of my eye I could see Aunt Titi looking nervously in my direction as she bustled about. At last the rush was over and I had made it through. I could not relax, however, as there was a weight in my stomach like lead.

Just as the last diners were leaving, Etienne came through the door. This was a surprise, he seldom came before evening. "Have you heard?" I asked.

"I have just returned from the hospital," he spoke softly, taking my hand and pressing it. "He is still barely conscious and weak from losing so much blood. They do not know yet if he will recover. They have telegraphed his brother in Paris. He is on his way to be with him now. I could not speak with him, he was sleeping, but they permitted me to sit by his bedside for a while. His condition is grave." And so Colette, my aunt and I stood around Etienne, clustered like a little circle of mourners. The somber words hung like a weighted shroud in the room.

"Come, Etienne," Aunt said. "Sit down for a minute. Tell us how he looked."

"He looked very pale and weak, but his breathing is steady. I talked to his doctor, Dr. Rey."

"Tell us, Etienne," Colette said somewhat impatiently, "what did the doctor say?"

"First and most important, he seemed rather hopeful. I was surprised, really. But he said he had seen similar cases with great loss of blood, and that Vincent was strong, really strong, and has the constitution of an ox. He said he has already been mumbling in his delirium about getting back to work. Then he said he had learned the house was stained everywhere with blood from Vincent's accident. It will have to be cleaned up before he can return . . . if indeed he recovers."

"And Gauguin?" I asked. "Where is Monsieur Gauguin?"

"He has not been seen. I guess he is still at the hotel, waiting for the brother to arrive."

Colette kept her eyes downcast, but I was furious. "When there is trouble, you can count on Monsieur Gauguin to run and hide. Poor Vincent, alone in the world."

"Etienne," Aunt Titi said. "You were kind to visit him."

"After his kindness to me, it seemed the least I could do. He is my friend. Postmaster Roulin has been also to visit." Etienne's face seemed lined with sadness.

In my mind, an idea was taking shape. Aunt Titi, Colette and I could go to the Little Yellow House and put it to rights. Then Vincent would feel better, knowing everything was clean and waiting for him when he was strong enough to return. Aunt Titi and Colette agreed. It was the proper thing to do.

"We'll go first thing in the morning," said my aunt. "Van Gogh gave me a spare key some time ago, in case he locked himself out. Poor creature. With no family here to call upon, we must do what we can."

*   *   *

The next day was Christmas day. How strange to be thinking of Vincent, lying in hospital, barely alive. I lay in my bed later that morning as we three had gone to midnight mass on Christmas Eve with Etienne, and of course the cafe was closed. I thought of my family in Saint Remy, they would already be awake, enjoying the Noel breakfast, preparing for a day of quiet leisure. Thank goodness the cafe was closed.

I spent a few minutes wondering what Noel would be like, after Etienne and I were married. Certainly we would be spending it with his mother, Pierre, Paul, Marguerite and little Paul. I wondered if we would be seeing the Roussilons quite so often and decided probably not. Agnes would focus her attention on someone else. Then my thoughts turned to Vincent, and I sprang out of bed and awakened Colette. There was much to be done.

*　　*　　*

The three of us, Aunt Titi, Colette and I, set out for the Little Yellow House shortly after noon. The streets of Arles were deserted. All of the shops were closed, of course. Hardly anyone was stirring as we made our way to Place Lamartine. The usual colony of young children was not even visible. "They must have eaten too many sugared almonds," Colette said nervously. She was very pale, and I knew she dreaded going to the place where Gauguin had so recently lived.

As we drew closer, a solitary man appeared walking toward us. I stared in disbelief, for I first thought it was Vincent. The blond hair, the tall figure and similar features. But of course it was not. This man was younger, his skin was pale, he had not been working in the fields. His hands looked white and soft. But something in the way he carried himself reminded me of Vincent. He walked past us, hardly seeing. He appeared to me to be a man with the weight of the world on his shoulders.

As we passed I saw his eyes—incredibly blue and weighted with sadness. Instantly I realized who he was. It was Theo, Vincent's brother. I turned and looked back, but he had already disappeared. This man was pale and ill, I thought. He had been walking in the direction of the train station. Could he be leaving? In our conversations together Vincent had spoken of his brother with affection. He wrote and received letters from him almost every day.

Wait, I remembered, Etienne had said he was expected in Arles. There was no doubt about it, that is who we saw. As we entered the Little Yellow House nobody spoke. I doubted Aunt Titi and Colette had noticed Vincent's brother.

What a disaster greeted us! The kitchen was full of dirty dishes, an overturned milk jug lay on its side, the contents oozing over the table top. I smelled the sour, curdled milk. Upstairs, Vincent's bedroom seemed covered in blood. The sheets and pillows were soaked, there were even smudges of blood on the walls. A trail of blood dripped all the way down the stairs to the front door. But strangely, the pictures on the walls were untouched.

Aunt set to work in the kitchen and Colette and I found a bucket and mop and went upstairs. First we took off the linens and cleaned the mattress and pillows as best we could. Then we hung clothes on pegs and tackled the walls and the floor, moving on down the stairs. Colette quickly bundled up the bed linens and went to the wash house, unmindful of what anyone would think about washing on Christmas Day.

"It is an act of mercy," Aunt said, "nobody would criticize that." She and I worked on in the other rooms until all was in good order in about an hour. We took a few minutes to admire the paintings. What a gallery that Little Yellow House had become! Those paintings were sacred to Vincent, I thought. They were his children.

Joined by Colette, we locked up the house, taking the freshly washed linens to dry on lines in the courtyard behind the cafe. As we were leaving Etienne joined us. He had gone to the hospital to pay Vincent a visit, but he was not able to see him as his condition was still very grave. His brother had been with him most of the day, leaving on the afternoon train to return to Paris. Etienne and Postmaster Roulin had sat outside his door for some time together. There was no sight and no word of Gauguin.

As Etienne and I walked behind Aunt and Colette, I whispered to him of the man we had met as we were walking toward the Little Yellow House. He told me he saw him also, leaving the hospital and walking alone toward Place Lamartine. We were sure then we had both seen Theo, Vincent's brother.

"I'll go for a visit tomorrow," Etienne said. "Vincent needs to know the Little Yellow House is clean and ready for his return."

CHAPTER SIXTEEN

But on December 27, Vincent suffered another serious attack. He would take no food and refused to talk with anyone. He spent a bad night and was put into an isolated room at the hospital. Etienne tried without success to visit Vincent.

Colette, meanwhile, made a quick post-Noel trip to Saint Remy. With great sadness she told me that Francine had been sick the whole time she was there, in bed with a fever. My hopes were dashed. It meant that she had not yet regained full health, even after food had become more plentiful. Was there no end to trouble in life, I thought, after one of the bleakest holidays I could remember.

Etienne showed his true colors through all of the hardship. Faithfully he went to see Vincent every day. Then he would come by to report to us at the cafe. Apparently Vincent's only other visitor was Postmaster Roulin, who was being transferred to a new posting in Marseilles. Etienne learned on one of his visits from Dr. Rey that Gauguin had returned to Paris at the same time Theo, the brother, left.

By early January, Etienne had brought us the news that Vincent had fully recovered. He was in good spirits and was moving freely about, and Etienne had walked with him about an hour in the courtyard of the hospital. Etienne pronounced his state of mind as healthy, anxious to leave the hospital and return to the Little Yellow House.

This encouraged us, so Aunt Titi and I planned to go the following day to visit Vincent before he was dismissed from the hospital. But early the next morning we received word from the Saint Remy farmer who gave us rides in his wagon that my mother asked me to come home. He said nothing about Francine but I knew she must have worsened.

Quickly I packed my valise at my aunt's bidding, embraced her and Colette, asking them to notify Etienne of the happenings, and I left for Saint Remy. I had so looked forward to this visit when I would share with my family the good news of my betrothal. But with every turn of the wagon wheels along the winter-barren landscape, all I could think of was my sister Francine. My fears grew with every mile, thinking of Francine, a prisoner of her weak body.

My mother met me at the door. And though I asked her at once how Francine was feeling, I already knew what her answer would be.

"She is not well. Her fever refuses to leave her. What she tries to swallow often comes up. The fever seems to subside for a few days, then it returns with renewed strength. I do not know what to do," she faltered, her lips trembling.

"Has the doctor seen her?"

"Seen her and done nothing," she answered scornfully. "He appears as much in the dark as I am. Come, let us go up. She has been longing to see you. That is why I asked you to come. I thought it might help her to get well."

Francine's little face was turned toward the door as we entered the room. Her eyes looked enormous in her small face which bore the ravages of some interior demon gnawing at her strength. She smiled when she saw me.

"Francine!" I gathered her pitiful little body into my arms and hugged her until I thought my heart would break. But I would not let her see anything but my happiness in being by her side.

*   *   *

Aunt Titi had told me to stay as long as I was needed. She would engage Edith to work both lunch and dinner times with Colette, and Colette had promised me to continue doing the cafe laundry. I was not to worry, they would manage without me. After I had been home one week, with little change in Francine's condition, I received two letters, one from Etienne and another from Vincent. Etienne wrote:

> Dear Minette,
>
> It seems like a month already that you have been away. I miss you so much! The municipal building is nearing completion, and they want to begin work on a second building as soon as it is finished. That should keep me in Arles for some time to come. It may delay our wedding, but that only means we will have more of a nest egg. I know that is important to you, but it means everything to me. I would not like to scrimp to keep a wife!
>
> My brother Pierre writes me that a farmer near us is thinking about selling his land. It is good, fertile land with vines and olive trees and a rich plot near the stream for growing vegetable crops. There is even a field of *lavandin*. The farmer has been successful in selling his lavender at the herb market in Aix-en-Provence. Unfortunately, the *mas* that goes with the land is hardly habitable, but it shows great promise, Pierre says. I will tell you now the worst: it has dirt floors! This means we would have to stay with *Maman* until I could put down tile floors and do some other work. Would that be too difficult for you?
>
> Of course we could postpone our wedding a year while

I get the house ready, but I do not wish to do that! I am
hoping you don't either! Not seeing you for just one week
has been hardship enough for me. I kiss your rosy cheeks
and your lovely eyes in my dreams.

Vincent is home now at the Little Yellow House. I will
let him tell you of his health, as he says he is writing you
today! Please give all there my love, especially *ma petite*
Mademoiselle Francine. I trust she will be well soon.

Your
Etienne

Vincent's letter sounded optimistic, as always. He wrote:

Dear Minette,

I have received permission of Etienne to write to you,
and I am hoping your sister Francine is improving. Tell her
not to lose hope, I know for a fact that the mind rules our
bodies and keeping a good attitude can work wonders!

Next I offer my sincere joy and best wishes upon your
betrothal. Etienne is one man in a million and you are a
pearl without price. Who can but predict happiness and
prosperity when two such fine people decide to unite!

With the help of Etienne and Postmaster Roulin, I
have returned to live in the Little Yellow House. They did
not know what to make of me in hospital, although good
Dr. Rey did his best. However, when they saw I was strong
enough in body, eating regularly, sleeping regularly and
making sense in my head, they knew it was time to let me
go. I do not know what came over me when I suffered the
attack when Gauguin left. I do not know the cause, and I
cannot be sure it will not happen again. I only know I must
get on with my life's work, Minette. I must seek the high
yellow note in my painting in the time I have left.

When I opened the door of my house I saw at once that ministering angels had been at work. I do not deserve such kindness, Minette, but I shall always be grateful to you, Madame Ginoux and Colette, for all your hard work on my behalf. It pains me that you found such a mess. Please know I was not myself when it happened.

My brother wants me to tell you also how grateful he is for all the help you kind friends have given me. So I am on my feet at last, working on one or two still lifes, one a wicker basket with lemons and oranges, then a cypress branch and a pair of blue gloves. You may have seen already some of my baskets of fruit. They are paintings for the time when the weather is too cold to venture out. How I long for the orchards to come into bloom!

I have painted another still life, my chair, the yellow ladderback, with my pipe and a packet of tobacco on the seat. I have also painted a self portrait. When you see it you will know that I have fully recovered. It is broadly painted in flat bands of orange and red and green and blue with yellow skin tones. It is as vigorous and as good as anything I have done yet. I am wearing a blue cap and a bandage over my poor ear.

As for reading, Minette, I hope you are keeping on with it so as to keep new ideas in your head. I have two more books for you when you return, one is "Uncle Tom's Cabin" by Harriet Beecher Stowe, a book on slavery that has been published for many years, but is one I never read. It is a powerful book. The other is Charles Dickens "A Christmas Carol."

At present the Reverend Salles, pastor of the Protestant church in Arles, is reading Mrs. Stowe's book. He should finish it soon. This man has been very kind to me. To any soul who has befriended me in my troubles, I am very grateful.

Please realize, Minette, that I shall be very happy when

your marriage to Etienne takes place. You deserve happiness
and security in a marriage such as Etienne will bring to you.
He is solid, dependable and hard working. And he is
captured completely by your charms! He speaks of you
constantly when he visits me. I too, speak to the Girl with
the Coffee-Tinted Skin as she hangs over my bed. I hope
you will write to me!

With warmest regards,
Vincent

As I reread the letter, I thought about the fear with which
Vincent struggled. Fear of more attacks . . . fear that the condition
was permanent . . . would become progressively worse. And yet,
he was not defeated. His love of life, his iron will were working
hand in hand to see him through. I had not met many priests who
possessed a belief in the goodness of life like Vincent did. Maybe,
just maybe, I could help my sister by coaxing her to think like
Vincent. I would try, with all my heart.

I went to Francine's room and began by reading Vincent's
letter to her. "You will see all these pictures he mentions for yourself.
Soon you will be well and we will go together to Arles. You will
meet Etienne again and this time you will meet Vincent. Think of
it, Francine! What a joy to journey to Arles in the spring!"

A spark of hope flickered in her eyes as she looked hungrily at
me. She is indeed hungry, hungry for life, I thought. In her face I
saw a child starving for life.

"Come, I'll fix an egg for your supper. We cannot have you not
eating! You must build up your strength so you will be strong for the
journey." Light flickered in those dark eyes. That night, she actually
finished the soft boiled egg and drank a glass of foaming milk.

"Look at you, you have a mustache now! I must call you
'Francois' now, not Francine." And she laughed, for the first time
since I'd arrived. I determined then to do everything I could to
raise her spirit and give her something to live for.

And she began to improve. It was as though she took strength from my assurances that she would begin to get better. My mother noticed the change in her immediately. Before long, she was out of her bed and sitting up in a chair.

"Of course, you know Etienne and I will be married soon, later in the year perhaps," I said, spinning happy pictures for her entertainment, "and I won't be able to stay home all day with Madame Martin. You must come for a visit to keep me company while Etienne is hard at work on the house he is getting ready.

"Yes, you must come to Nimes and together we will pick the lavender and make lavender bags together to send to Mother and to Aunt Titi. Maybe, if she is very nice, we will send one to Colette!" At this we both laughed, remembering Colette's sly ways.

"We will grow tomatoes as big as coffee cups, you and I, then, in the evenings, when Etienne is there, Madame Martin will take down the *santons* and we will look at them. They are so beautiful, Francine."

And so we spent the days. I made her happy with tales of part fantasy, part truth and at the same time feeding her soft boiled eggs, tiny morsels of ham, bread and butter with glasses of milk. And remarkably, she did improve. The fever disappeared as mysteriously as it had come and she gained a little weight. Francine would never be robust, but her will to live got her out of bed and on her feet, though still she was frail and needed much care.

"A miracle!" exclaimed my mother to me as we sat together after Francine had gone to sleep for the night. And I began to make plans to return to Arles and to try to persuade my mother to let Francine accompany me for a visit of one week.

First of all, I wrote Aunt Titi. Francine could sleep in my cot and I would sleep in the one unoccupied since Gisele had left. Francine would rest a lot while I worked, and she would enjoy watching the bustle of the cafe. I knew my aunt would be agreeable to the plan, and she could easily persuade my mother to part with her youngest, just for a week.

CHAPTER SEVENTEEN

Thursday, February 7, arrived, our departure date. Francine had improved enough to make the journey. I planned that her time in Arles would be a week of pampering from Colette, Aunt Titi and me.

There was a *mistral* wind blowing as the farmer pulled up at our house, the back of the wagon filled with chickens he planned to sell in Arles. The sky looked threatening as though it might rain. But the weather was mild, almost feeling like spring.

"I don't like the look of that sky a little bit," he said to my mother, who was fussing anxiously over Francine, fastening her bonnet securely.

"Surely it will be sunny later in the day," she said. "If only the wind would stop blowing."

Nothing could quell our high spirits as we rolled away from Saint Remy. To Francine, the trip was the biggest adventure of her life, and I was determined to make her happy. But by the time we passed through the village of Fontvielle it had begun to rain. The farmer stopped the wagon and pulled an old oilcloth from under the wagon seat and draped it over us.

Francine sat in the middle with the farmer and I on either side, as a buffer from the rain. He continually urged the horse on, but we were moving at a snail's pace. The poor beast, blinded and frightened by the rain's intensity and maddened by the shrieking *mistral*, refused to do more than creep along. Finally the horse stopped altogether.

A huge tree had fallen across the road. The horse could go no farther. Just ahead we could barely make out a shed of some sort by the road. We climbed down and hurried toward it in the downpour. Lightning was flashing all around us. Pushing at the flimsy door I more or less fell inside with Francine falling in behind me. The farmer shouted that he would see to his horse and the chickens and disappeared into the storm.

"Minette, I am so frightened!" Francine said, her teeth chattering with cold. I felt great shivers going through her body and I flung my cape over her and left her side to search out in the semi-darkness whatever shelter might be in the shed, an old bed, some blankets, perhaps a chair.

At that moment I heard an earsplitting crash and saw a flash of brilliant light followed by a loud cracking sound. Then blackness. That was all I remembered.

*   *   *

I woke up in a bed weighted with eiderdown, my eyes unaccustomed to the rosy light of a lamp. With a start, I recognized objects of Aunt Titi's room. But what was I doing in her bed? "Where am I?" I called out.

"Shhh, *ma petite*," came my aunt's voice from somewhere near the bed. "Go to sleep. You have had a tremendous shock." And I did go back to sleep, drowsily burrowing into the welcoming warmth of the eiderdown. Later, I never remembered seeing my aunt, only hearing her voice, assuring me, calming me before I slept again.

The next time I awoke, bright sunlight was shining in the room and Colette and Aunt were peering anxiously into my face. "What has happened? Why am I here?" I asked, my mouth feeling dry and cotton-like, my head aching.

"You are here in my bed, Minette, because you were in a horrible storm and a tree was struck by lightning and fell on the shed where you had gone for shelter." Colette's face looked pale and drawn. My aunt's face was deathly white.

Desperately my mind groped back to that fierce storm, the horse refusing to move, the flimsy door of the shed giving way as I pushed on it. Francine! I tried to sit up. Where was Francine? As I looked into the faces of my sister and my aunt I felt a frantic fear like nothing I had ever known before.

"Where is she?" I whispered, my voice sounding like a stranger's, I was so weak.

"Francine has left us, *ma petite*. She is dead." And with terrible finality, my aunt made the sign of the cross, her eyes glistening with tears. It could not be true. I looked quickly at my sister who was standing quietly beside me, tears streaming down her cheeks. She nodded slightly. I fell back on the covers. "Tell me."

Colette began to speak in a dull, dead sounding voice. "The farmer went to secure the horse and wagon, leaving you both inside the shed. At that moment a huge tree next to the shed was struck by lightening and fell, flattening the shed and falling directly on Francine. The trunk narrowly missed you but you were struck in the head by a falling timber. Francine was not so lucky. She died instantly. She felt no pain, it was so sudden. The farmer managed to get help and brought you here. You were only a short distance from Arles. *Maman* is arriving presently."

"No," I screamed, "This could not happen. Francine was getting so much better. She was stronger! She cannot be dead."

"Hush, Minette," Aunt Titi's voice tried to soothe. "Who knows why these things happen? The one who rules over us has his reasons. We must not question! She is now with the angels, free of all suffering."

"But she was much improved," I cried. "She was getting better and she was so happy! For the first time she believed she would get well. I encouraged her and helped her. Now I am alive and she is gone!"

"Don't blame yourself, Minette," Colette said softly. "Do not reproach yourself. I know Francine loved you best and that she died happy because she was with you. You made her happy to the end."

I tried to throw off the covers and get out of bed. But there was a shooting pain in my arm. They told me I sprained it, trying to move the timber off my body. My head was pounding and felt heavy as a cannon ball. Helpless, I lay back and tears rolled out of the side of my closed lids as I realized finally that there was nothing, really nothing, that I could do.

*   *   *

The days melted one into another as I lay in bed, listless, unable to stir myself. I remember my mother at my bedside, crying softly as she held my hand, murmuring "Gone, gone, my baby is gone. Minette, Minette, what shall I do?" Then it was much later and she had left, and it was the figure of Edith I made out, moving quietly about. She must have been put in charge while the others went to the funeral in Saint Remy.

Dimly I was aware of Edith caring for me, spooning a bit of broth between my teeth, trying to brush out my hair on the pillow. To tell the truth, I cared little whether I lived or died. All I could think of was that if I hadn't insisted, Francine would not have been in the wagon that day on the way to Arles. And she would be alive. Over and over this thought turned in my brain. I could not expel it, try as I would.

The funeral mass was over. Etienne had accompanied my mother, Colette and Aunt Titi to Saint Remy where my brothers were waiting. Edith kept looking in on me as she and Monsieur Raspail tried to keep the cafe going. My wounds were healing, my sprained arm almost mended, but still I lay there, numb and unfeeling.

Once I glimpsed myself in the mirror of my aunt's bedroom. Eyes like two large gray mushrooms stared out at me. My hair hung rank and untended. My cheeks had no color. A pitiful sight I was. It would take a jolt to bring me to my senses.

*   *   *

Every day since the accident, Etienne had been to visit me but I would not go downstairs to see him. He had brought me small bouquets of flowers, but still I could not force myself to get out of bed. Then one evening Etienne did not come. Instead, I heard a loud voice below saying, "Tell her if she does not come down in five minutes, I am coming up to talk to her! I must speak to her!"

In a panic, I threw back the bedcoverings and hurried to my wardrobe, seized the first dress I could see and put it over my head. I hastily washed my face in the hand basin and reached for the hairbrush. I could not bear the thought of anyone seeing me lying in the rumpled bed, unwashed and untidy. I hurried downstairs and found Vincent.

"Pardon my appearance, Vincent. You should not have to pay a call to me. It is I who should be visiting you! Are you well?" I was filled with shame. For the first time, I began to see how selfish I had been.

"You have suffered a great sorrow," he said. "I understand that. But do you know others also are suffering? Your sister, your aunt and Etienne? All of them are grieving too."

"Vincent," I raised my eyes to his and he took my hands, "I feel so sad. My grief is like a millstone around my neck. I cannot be free of it!"

"Hush, Minette," he said softly. We were in full view of the dining room and I could see inquisitive eyes looking at us. "I understand. Of course you must mourn for your sister, but life must go on. We must fulfill our purpose, each in his own way. Mine is my painting. Yours is to help your mother and your sister and your aunt all of whom are bowed down in grief. Then there is Etienne. He has borne your burden as though he was already a

member of your family. He needs you now. You must realize that."
He paused.

"Francine would not wish you to withdraw from the world, you know she would not."

"Of course, Vincent, you are right." I was thinking how he had not let misfortune weigh him down. He was rising up time after time. Thinking of him I felt truly humble.

"Will you tell Etienne I wish to see him?" I asked.

"Of course," he said. "And soon, when the weather settles, the three of us will go to Montmajour abbey for a picnic. We will celebrate the arrival of the springtime and I will paint the orchards and you and Etienne will plan your wedding. There is so much to live for!"

After that meeting with Vincent, I returned to the world. How could I not, with such an example as Vincent urging me to choose life?

*   *   *

Several days after I had resumed my duties and life was back to normal, Etienne told me what had happened to Vincent during the time I had been in Saint Remy.

"He suffered another bad attack of the madness on the very afternoon you left for Saint Remy. You remember, your aunt had planned that day to visit him. For three days he was dangerously ill. At the hospital, the doctor in charge told me he suffered from hallucinations and heard voices reproaching him, and that he was constantly afraid of being poisoned.

"When he returned home again, he felt better, but by then the neighborhood was aroused by a few troublemakers who claimed that it was dangerous for him to live on Place Lamartine, even though he was sleeping at the hospital and taking his meals there."

"Etienne, how horrible! Above all else, Vincent loves the Little Yellow House. His lifework is there. How can he hope to live without his work?"

"That is not the worst of it, Minette. Thirty of the people in the area have signed a petition to the mayor, claiming that Vincent is not in possession of his mental faculties, that he drinks too much, that he is a threat to women and children. He should therefore, they say, be returned to his family, or be placed in an institution."

I could not believe it. That they could say such things of the calm, reasonable man who recently paid me a call and was responsible for bringing me to my senses! "Etienne, this is madness of the worst sort."

"And so, Minette, just today, the mayor acted on the petition. The police took Vincent to the hospital to be readmitted, and put locks on the Little Yellow House."

"What a horror. Vincent is not mad! He would not hurt anyone, only himself. Can't they see that?"

"And there is his side of the story also," Etienne continued. "He says the children of the neighborhood mock him and taunt him on the street, actually come up to the windows of his house looking in and shouting until it becomes unbearable." Here Etienne paused and rubbed his hands together.

"Such goading would try the patience of a saint," I said.

Thinking of the women I had seen at the wash house, I could well imagine Mauricette leading some of her weaker friends to sign such a petition. Small minded people are always suspicious of anyone who is different. And they had all apparently lined up against Vincent.

"Etienne," I said, "we must do something for him."

"Yes, I agree," he said, "but I'm not sure we can do anything at this point. As long as he is isolated in hospital we cannot see him. We must wait until he improves. Then we can perhaps decide what to do."

As we sat together thinking of Vincent, Etienne spoke again. "I will check each day at the hospital for news of his condition, while you, Minette, must rejoin your world again. Too many of us need you."

*   *   *

After a healthy dose of reality from both Vincent and Etienne, I returned to the routine of the cafe, working harder than ever to show my aunt that I was really sorry for all the trouble I had caused.

How lucky our family was to have Aunt Titi. Not even a blood relation, she was supportive and loyal. She was also generous, her kindness of the past year had held our family together. I tried to tell her this awkwardly one day as we sat resting after the rush of noontime.

"Nonsense, child," she said quickly. "You have no idea how I suffered after your uncle died. The loneliness would have been unbearable had not your mother and father supported me. Now you are my family. I consider you and Colette like the girls I never had! And your mother is like a true sister to me."

Suddenly I felt I had the strength to ask her what I had been longing to know. "Aunt, will you tell me what Francine's funeral was like?"

She was silent for a moment as she arranged her thoughts. Finally she spoke, telling me everything in greatest detail. About the mourners, that Francine looked truly peaceful and beautiful and that her face was not at all marred. She told me how the priest's words brought true comfort to my mother and everyone else in that grieving body of mourners. She told me of how kind and helpful Etienne was, how my brothers helped my mother as she walked behind the coffin to the graveyard. She described the flowers in great detail. She told me that the priest was kind, returning to our house after the service ended, how his words comforted my mother and all who were present.

That talk with my aunt turned my thoughts forward. After hearing her words, I was somehow at peace. I could look back on my precious Francine and be grateful for our times together. But at the same time I was now ready to face whatever life would bring.

CHAPTER EIGHTEEN

Slowly I mended from the overwhelming grief of Francine's death. It helped being surrounded by people who loved me, my aunt and my sister and Etienne. Vincent was not so fortunate, I thought. Alone, verbally attacked by hostile neighbors on Place Lamartine, he was unequal to the strain.

First, his hopes for a companion in Gauguin were dashed. Then word came to him that Theo was planning to be married. As much as Vincent tried to rejoice at the news, he immediately realized his own status would change. No longer would he be Theo's primary concern. Theo would soon have a wife to look after. This new worry weighed on the delicate balance of his mental state.

After the neighbors circulated the petition against Vincent, the Reverend Salles felt it would be unwise for Vincent to return to the Little Yellow House and face the animosity. Dr. Rey agreed, and so it was arranged for Vincent to live at the hospital, the *Hotel Dieu*. They told him his house had been locked up by the police. Inside were all of his paintings and the supplies he needed to work. It was an impossible situation.

Etienne and I discussed the problem of Vincent every night when Etienne came to the cafe. I felt Vincent should not give up the Little Yellow House. It was important to his recovery that he understand it would be waiting for him. Etienne was not so sure. "He is not strong enough mentally to face up to the neighbors, Minette," Etienne said. "Remember, he has had several of these attacks since the first one at Noel. They have left him in a much more fragile mental state."

"But he put so much of himself into the house," I answered. "The house is the symbol of his hopes and dreams that sent him to Arles in the first place. The paintings, the furniture, the special sunflower paintings. They have been such an inspiration to him."

In the end, however, I saw the logic of Etienne's words. Vincent was being held a prisoner at the hospital by the vengeful neighbors. Perhaps he could rent a small place in another part of town and start over, then he would stand a better chance of working in peace.

*   *   *

Vincent surprisingly appeared at the cafe one day with an artist friend from Paris. It was some time since we had seen him and he told us he had his canvas and his paints back again and was beginning to work. He was allowed to leave the hospital during the day, but was taking his meals and sleeping there.

He introduced his friend, the artist Paul Signac, to us. I liked this tall, thin, gentle man. He was mild-mannered and courteous. His eyes were filled with kindness and he seemed genuinely glad to meet some of Vincent's friends. He also seemed to be concerned for Vincent.

"Paul is on his way to Cassis to paint for a while," said Vincent, proud as a new parent of the friend he had brought to us.

"Theo Van Gogh told me in Paris where I could find Vincent," Signac added, "We are on our way now to the Little Yellow House so I can look at Vincent's work."

I thought Vincent seemed almost like himself. He did not appear to be under a strain and was clearly pleased at the visit.

What a shame, I thought, that Signac hadn't arrived to stay at the Little Yellow House instead of Gauguin. I remembered also thinking, "Maybe this horrible ordeal for Vincent is coming to an end. Maybe he is stable enough to take up painting again as before."

The next day Signac left, after a morning walk around the town in the company of Vincent. His visit seemed to do Vincent a lot of good. After Signac had left, Vincent invited Etienne and me to go with him on a painting expedition to the orchards in bloom on the next Sunday afternoon.

We did not go as far as Montmajour abbey. I think Vincent realized it was probably too far for him in his weakened state. It would dissipate too much of his precious energy, energy he needed for painting. Instead, he chose a small orchard on the outskirts of Arles, far away from Place Lamartine.

It was a glorious spring day, one of those three hundred days of sunshine we are credited as having in Provence each year. Aunt had presented me with a new dress. Not a fine gown, of course, it was only a dress for everyday, but the print was soft, white flowers on a green ground. It was lovely and springlike.

I liked the way Etienne kept glancing at me as we walked along. Vincent told us he had heard from Signac. He had written that he was astounded at the power of Vincent's work and urged him to keep painting.

"Such praise will swell your head, Vincent," Etienne joked.

"Do not jest, friend," Vincent replied, his smile sad. "Such words to me are like water to a man dying of thirst in the desert!"

I spread a small cloth and we shared wine and bread and cheese, but Vincent would not stop painting to eat. I can see him in my mind to this day at the easel, his long fingers around the brush, stroking the canvas liberally with paint as he took bites from a wedge of cheese grasped in his other hand. The blue fire of his eyes kindled my thoughts: Let him be free of whatever demons possess him. Let him be free to paint like this!

It was time for us to be going back. At this time, Vincent was still spending the nights in hospital, although during the day he was free to go about painting the orchards, wherever he could find some that were not far from the town. It occurred to me that it was Dr. Rey who had set the limits on how far Vincent could travel. But Vincent never said anything about it to me.

Early in April Postmaster Roulin came for a final visit with Vincent at the hospital. He had been working in Marseilles since January. Now he had returned to move his family to their new home.

Roulin had been a true friend to Vincent. He had painted Roulin, his wife Augustine and her new baby, over and over again. He had painted the couple's older son. I knew the sadness Vincent must be feeling to lose one of his few loyal friends and supporters in Arles.

*   *   *

Pierre, Etienne's brother, wrote that he had successfully completed the purchase of the adjoining farm near Nimes on Etienne's behalf. Etienne had visited the property several times, and I could tell he was itching to get back to tilling the earth. Pierre and *Maman* had loaned Etienne what money he lacked to make the purchase.

The work had begun in earnest on the second municipal building in Arles, and Etienne was put in charge of a group of joiners. This pleased him, for it meant that he would be earning more francs. The men liked working for him. He always expected their best, but he was fair.

It looked as though we could be getting married in the summer.

*   *   *

At the cafe, I began to enjoy my work, for the first time since my sister's death. Colette and I worked well together, and Aunt Titi said we could do the work of three girls, especially as Edith was on hand to step in when we needed her. Edith recently had confided in me that she was expecting a child in September, although she had not yet told my aunt.

One day after a slow lunch hour, I was straightening up a bit, preparing the room for the evening. Aunt had gone upstairs with Colette, who announced her intention of shampooing her hair. I knew my aunt would take her usual short afternoon nap. Alone, enjoying the quiet, I folded napkins, shook out cloths, and lined up chairs to the tables.

There was a faint tap at the window and I looked up. Gisele! In the grief and confusion of all that had happened, I'd almost forgotten Gisele. I hurried to let her in.

"Gisele, it is good to see you. Come in."

Nervously she made her way inside. "I looked in and saw that you were alone. I wanted to speak with you. I did not feel I could face your aunt."

"Nonsense, Gisele. Aunt is very fond of you. You know she was terribly upset when you left. Every day she hoped you would come back." Gisele looked unconvinced.

"I am certain she did not approve of where I went. She must have hated it."

Her gaze lowered; she examined her hands.

"Now, Gisele, I know, and Aunt Titi knows too, that you had your reasons. It is not our place to judge others."

"Oh, Minette, if you could only understand how lonely I was!" Her eyes pleaded with me. "There was no one I could confide in. You and Edith were so much quicker and cleverer than I was. And when Colette came after Edith left, it was worse. I felt ever so stupid. She could serve rings around me." Sadly I realized what she said was true, and we had largely ignored Gisele. The awareness of it hurt.

"And is that why you left?"

She hesitated a bit. "Loneliness was the main reason," she said, biting her lower lip. "I had met the woman who, ah, manages the place where I am now, at the baker's shop. She was friendly to me and took the time to speak to me. Nobody else ever gave me the time of day." I felt my cheeks redden. Edith, Colette and I had a lot to answer for, I thought.

"Oh, I'm not blaming you, Minette," she said, seeing my embarrassed glances in her direction. "You had your own family to take up your time. Anyway, Madame Clotilde told me one day that they needed someone to run errands, go to the baker, the butcher, that sort of thing. She said she would look out for me and treat me like one of her own children. I . . . I do not have any family, Minette. What she said meant so much to me." She paused, waiting for my reaction.

"I understand, Gisele, I truly do."

"There is something else I want you to know, Minette," she said. "I . . . I do not have visitors at the house. I had to register with the police, everyone living there does that, but I am not a hostess." The look in the brown eyes was one of pride. Even Gisele had her scruples, I thought, as I took her hand.

"Of course, Gisele," I said faintly. "I understand. And is this job giving you all you were hoping to find?"

"You won't understand me, Minette, but in a strange way, it is. I still haven't any close friends, but the girls are decent to me. Madame Clotilde is kind to me. We talk sometimes. The other girls tell me their troubles. It is not a family of course, but in a funny kind of way, it is a family . . . of sorts."

The realization that this girl had found kindness and acceptance of a sort that never showed itself as she worked at the cafe made me uneasy. I had never thought of life in a *Maison de Tolerance* as having that quality. I was somewhat humbled by it.

"And do you ever think of leaving?" I asked.

"Where would I go?" she replied. "No respectable restaurant would hire me if they knew. Even if I said I was not a hostess, nobody would believe me." I thought of Colette, and how her sharp mind had guessed at the time of her disappearance, the truth of what Gisele was now saying.

Gisele continued to stand there with lowered eyes, twisting her handkerchief in both of her hands. "Monsieur Vincent has been a great help to me," she said surprisingly. My thoughts flew back to the time when he told Aunt Titi of Gisele's whereabouts. So he had kept up with her and offered her kindness. My feelings of discomfort grew.

"He has been a good friend," she continued. "Always asking to see me, to visit a few minutes when he calls in."

"I see," I said, feeling more uncomfortable.

"You must not think ill of him, Minette," Gisele said quickly, misreading my look. "He is a lonely person too."

"And what about the episode on Christmas Eve?" I asked, my curiosity getting the better of me. She hesitated a minute before answering.

"Minette, it was horrible. Never in my life have I been so frightened. The man who did that could not have been Vincent, but it was! At that moment, on that night, someone completely at odds with him was inside his body. When I was with the Sisters, in Montpelier, we had readings daily from the Scriptures. They often read to us of Jesus driving demons out of people. That is what Van Gogh was like on Christmas Eve. He was a man possessed by a demon."

Poor Gisele, and yet she had a strength about her that I envied somehow. Who can say they would have had her courage to act as she did when given the opportunity to go to a place among those who cared for her? And she had analyzed Vincent's condition as well as any of the doctors. They were baffled too. And she certainly was not one to judge others. I stood up as she gathered up her parcels and prepared to leave.

"Please wait, Gisele. At least let me call down Aunt Titi and Colette."

"No, Minette. It is better this way. Tell them I send my best wishes. Tell your aunt I thank her for all her kindness to me, especially the box of sugared almonds. I cried when I unpacked my things and saw them. They were the first present I ever received in my entire life, Minette."

Surely we of the world had a lot to answer for with so many

souls walking around in misery like Gisele. I thanked her for coming and urged her to stop by again for a talk. But I doubted she would do it. She had found a welcoming place in her world and we both knew I had missed an opportunity to befriend her once. I would not get another chance.

After she left I thought of several things I could have said to bring Gisele comfort. But when I told Aunt Titi, all she said was, "Humph! That girl has ruined herself!" Colette however, looked thoughtful and said nothing. She had learned life can indeed turn ugly, as it had in her encounter with Gauguin.

CHAPTER NINETEEN

At long last Vincent, who was still living at the hospital and going out days to paint, realized toward the end of April that he was not going to be able to return to the Little Yellow House. He stored his furniture in Aunt Titi's garret and began the job of crating his pictures to send them off to Theo in Paris.

Etienne helped him with this task and told me that Vincent was heartbroken that his precious paintings were being sent away and the Little Yellow House dismantled. However, he realized it was inevitable, and tried to put a brave face on it. He is sending away his children, I thought. That is how he sees his pictures.

"One of the paintings was flaking badly," Etienne said, "and we had to stick newspapers on to it. Some of the pictures have been spoiled by moisture during Vincent's absence. When the Rhone flooded earlier, it came within a few feet of his doorway on Place Lamartine. On top of that, the house had no inside fires all the time Vincent was away. While we were working with the packing, Minette, the walls were oozing water and saltpeter."

So necessity had driven Vincent to abandon his intransigence and act. As a gesture of thanks for Etienne's help, Vincent invited Etienne and me for a meal the coming Sunday afternoon, at a local boardinghouse where he sometimes went to eat when the hospital food and surroundings became too depressing.

They had worked together, sending off two full crates of pictures to Paris, storing the furniture with Aunt Titi and finally, Etienne accompanied Vincent to the landlord, where he turned over the key to Number Two, Place Lamartine.

Etienne told me that Vincent had decided to rent a small apartment from Dr. Rey in another part of town, a place he could use as a studio and as a storage place for paintings, with the hope that soon he might be well enough to live there permanently. But it was smaller, furnished sparsely, and not nearly so spacious as the Little Yellow House.

I was hopeful as we walked to join Vincent at the boardinghouse. I thought the meal would be a celebratory one, that he would be telling us that he was leaving the hospital for good, to go to the new apartment. Etienne, however remained silent and did not speculate.

We saw Vincent waiting at the entrance. He was wearing a new suit he had purchased recently. His hair and beard had been trimmed. He looked surprisingly neat. Even the indelible stains of paint which covered his hands had been carefully scrubbed.

He apologized for the early hour. "You know they expect me back by dark at the hospital," he said. "All in all, they have been very good to me. I won't let them down."

The boardinghouse was tired looking. with faded wallpaper of a paisley design that seemed to undulate on the walls. Two framed photographs of the *Pont du Gard*, the *Arc de Triomphe* and an embarrassingly bad painting of a field of cows completed the wall decorations. The furniture was as one would expect, slippery horsehair sofas that were badly sprung with crocheted antimacassars on backs and arms. Two worn fireside chairs stood near a large round table which held a few tattered periodicals. Beyond the oak double doors was the dining room. The air was redolent with cooking smells, past and present.

We entered the dining room where some twenty people were seated at a long table already eating. Vincent seated me with a flourish at a small table set up for three facing the room's one window. I faced the window, with Vincent and Etienne sitting on either side of me. The view, though unconventional, was beautiful. A large plane tree near the house covered the window with fresh new green leaves which shimmered in the late sunlight.

The meal was a happy one, in spite of our being in a room with the noise of strangers seated at the long table, and indifferent food, either overcooked or undercooked. Etienne and I drank a glass of wine, while Vincent drank milk. A large pitcher of foaming milk was placed at his side by Madame Rouen, the owner, who attended our table. Vincent had become a favorite of hers, she told us as she served us. Presently she left us alone.

As we ate, Vincent demanded to know more of our wedding plans. "It seems weddings are in style now," he said. "My brother has now entered the married state. My sister-in-law is a Dutch girl he met in Paris. Can it be that there is still hope for me, Minette?" he smiled and I recalled our past conversations about marriage. But I saw that Vincent's eyes were not smiling. He seemed somewhat withdrawn, taut inside, wound up, but at the same time he was playing the role of genial host for all it was worth.

Etienne told him we had decided to hold our wedding in Nimes, in deference to his mother, who was too frail to travel anymore. Privately I wondered about this, as it was much more logical to hold the wedding there because the *mas* was large and comfortable, much easier to accommodate wedding guests than at my mother's small house in Saint Remy would have been. Whatever the true reason, I was grateful for Etienne's tact in suggesting it.

As twilight took the place of sunlight, we finished our coffee. The room was deserted now but for a pair of older men reading periodicals in a far corner. Vincent began speaking to us in a low voice.

""I have been in Arles over a year now, not quite a year and a half. In many ways, it has been the most productive time of my painting life."

"And this year will be the best yet, Vincent," I added, "Now you can begin getting the new apartment ready to move in."

"Ah, Minette, you always are encouraging me! But it will not be quite like that." Quietly Etienne put his hand over mine as Vincent spoke.

"You see, Minette, I am leaving Arles. My time here has come to an end."

"Leaving? Whatever do you mean?" Feelings of dismay and forboding ran through me.

"I have made great improvement since the Christmas Eve episode," he answered carefully. "But there have been several attacks since that time. You know that. These attacks are horrible, Minette. I have frightening dreams and hallucinations. These are so dreadful I cannot bear to think about them, even long after they are over. Therefore I have asked to be given a place at Saint Paul de Mausole, the asylum in Saint Remy. There is a Dr. Peyron there who thinks he can help me. My brother and Dr. Rey and the Reverend Salles— all of them think this is best for me, and that is my wish. Good Etienne here knows the situation and he too feels I should do what I believe is best." Here he stopped to sip the last of his coffee as I tried to assimilate everything Vincent was saying.

"I have exchanged several letters with Dr. Peyron and so has my brother. He has promised to give me two rooms, one for sleeping and one for working. This of course means everything to me, Minette. Without work, I cannot live."

So Vincent had already confided in Etienne and this explanation was for my benefit. I could not keep the shock, the surprise, the horror out of my eyes. When I finally spoke my voice sounded dead, without inflection of any kind.

"But, but haven't you been continuing to improve? I thought you were looking better, eating better . . ." My voice trailed off.

"It is what I had hoped for most in the world, Minette," Vincent said sadly, looking into my eyes. "The truth of the matter is, I am not strong enough to live alone any more. I must have help."

Wildly my thoughts ran to Aunt and Colette. Could he not live at the cafe, and we look after him? What would be wrong with that? But in my heart, I knew it could not happen.

Vincent, as though reading my thoughts, spoke very gently and quietly to me in that faded room. "I am not what I seem to you, Minette. Haven't I always told you of my other side, my dark side?"

"Yes, but surely . . ."

"Minette, listen." His voice had an urgency and at the same time held great sorrow. "Unless I am watched over I do not eat properly, sleep proper hours. And what is infinitely worse, I drink turpentine and eat tubes of paint when the terrors inhabit me. I must have strong supervision. That is why I am going to Saint Remy, in the hope that I may be cured."

So there I had it, in Vincent's own words. The attacks had become progressively worse, and they were becoming more frequent. Logically, reasonably, Vincent was fighting for his very survival. But I could not keep from my mind the recurring rumors I'd heard about the place where Vincent was going to seek a cure for the unspeakable attacks he suffered.

"Saint Paul de Mausole, the sanitarium. That is a holding pen for the demented." Or, "If you aren't mad when you go in, you will be mad when you come out!" That is what I had heard from the townspeople in Saint Remy. And I had heard children at school whisper of the horrible cries of the patients issuing forth from the windows. It was too dreadful to contemplate. I pushed those thoughts away, and willed myself talk of happier times as we left the boardinghouse and walked with Vincent toward the hospital.

The porter opened the door and I turned to Vincent and put my arms around his neck. "Dear Vincent, you are precious to us. Our thoughts go with you. Come back to us as soon as you can."

I could see the blue eyes misted as he stepped inside. "*Au Revoir*, good friends. Until we meet again."

*   *   *

Vincent's departure for the asylum shocked Aunt Titi and Colette. He made the fifteen mile journey by train accompanied by the Reverend Salles. When Vincent came by the cafe on the way to the railway station to tell us goodbye, he asked Aunt to continue to store his furniture for him until he could make other arrangements. Aunt took both of his hands and warmly assured him that she would be happy to do so. She told him solemnly that he was a good friend and that he could always be sure of his good friends at the Cafe Ginoux in Arles.

Colette also gave him an emotional farewell. Since the trouble with Gauguin when Vincent had helped her so much, she considered Vincent a loyal friend. I could not keep back the tears as I told Vincent goodbye. This departure filled me with fear. I could not help it.

I wrote to my mother about Vincent. She was shocked as we all were, especially as she had grave suspicions about the asylum of Saint Paul de Mausole. She promised me she would visit him. It was after May 20 that my first letter from Vincent arrived. This is what he wrote:

Dear Minette,

Gradually I am settling into my new life here in Saint Remy. Did you know that Saint Paul's is an old Augustinian monastery? My room is a little room papered in greenish gray with curtains of sea green with a design of pale roses, brightened by touches of blood red. These curtains are very pretty in design. The room has a worn armchair. It has a cover splashed over like a Diaz or a Monticelli painting with brown, red, pink, white, cream, black, forget-me-not blue and bottle green.

Through the iron-barred window I see a square field of wheat in an enclosure, a perspective like van Goyen, the

Dutch painter of the seventeenth century, above which I see the morning sun rising in all its glory. Beside this room, I have another one to work in.

The food is so-so. Normally it tastes rather moldy, as in a cockroach-infested restaurant in Paris, or in a boardinghouse. These poor souls living here do absolutely nothing—not a book, nothing to distract them but a game of bowls and a game of checkers. They have no daily occupation other than to stuff themselves with chickpeas, beans, lentils and other groceries and merchandise from the colonies in fixed quantities and at regular hours.

The fear of madness is leaving me to a great extent as I see at close quarters those who are affected by it in the same way as I may easily be in the future. I intend to go on quietly, and may have a better idea of my future at the end of a year.

I am working on four canvases of the garden and two or three drawings. Yesterday I drew a death's head moth, a beautiful creature. It was a pity I had to kill it in order to paint it.

Minette, forgive my self-centered ramblings. I long to see you and Etienne. To have a lively discussion with you about one of Zola's novels would please me beyond measure. Tell Etienne I will send a letter to him soon.

Yours,
Vincent

I had never known anyone in my entire life like Vincent. Faced with such insurmountable difficulties, he was able to keep up his spirits. Truthfully he had told me about conditions in the asylum. The straightforward letter let me know that Vincent was not sunk in despair. On the contrary, he was looking at his situation coolly and with logic.

As he had always done in his painting, he now applied his intellect to his mental state. I cringed, thinking of how he must feel hearing the cries and ravings of the insane who surrounded him. But Vincent wrote that the fear of madness was leaving him! Now that he was surrounded by it, he better understood it I surmised.

Feeling that I could best help Vincent in this way, I sent him a new novel to read. It was by a writer called Edouard Rod, *Le Sens de la Vie.* I read it first, enjoyed it and sent it to him, hoping it would be one he liked. Almost immediately, in a letter to Etienne, he thanked me for it and said he had begun to reread it.

Of course Etienne and I shared our letters from Vincent. Etienne's work in Arles was coming to an end. As soon as the second municipal building was finished, a much smaller one than the first, Etienne would leave for Nimes. He was anxious to get on his own land, to begin renovations to the *mas* that would be our home.

"Etienne," I asked one evening as we strolled toward the arena after the cafe had closed, "tell me what you truly think about Vincent's condition." He waited for a minute before replying.

"I think it is a condition that can probably be overcome," he answered carefully, "but in order to do so the patient needs to be free of all anxieties and worries, to have loving support from a family, and be able to follow the physician's orders to the letter."

In many ways it was not a comforting answer.

CHAPTER TWENTY

July. Thoughts of my wedding were uppermost in my mind. Etienne was preparing to leave for Nimes. We had set the wedding for August thinking he would have completed the most pressing work on his land and I would have my preparations complete. My primary concern at the moment was about the dress I would wear. I had spoken to Etienne of my wishes in the frankest way.

"My family are plain people, hard working, no thought of putting on airs. I would like our wedding to be simple, Etienne, with only our families present, if that would be possible. And I don't want to wear a wedding dress of silk or satin. Just something summer-like and simple. That would suit me best."

"Exactly my wishes," Etienne said with great relief. "I will write *Maman* at once. I do not want our wedding to be a carnival side show. Your ideas sound perfect."

Before he wrote the letter, the very next day in fact, a letter came from Nimes addressed to both of us. It was from Agnes Roussilon.

"What can she be writing us about," Etienne exclaimed in dismay. "Agnes has followed me about like a gadfly for years." There was exasperation in his voice.

"Wait, Etienne, let's see what she says. Do not be so quick to judge." Etienne opened the letter and we read:

Dear Minette and Etienne,

Congratulations on your betrothal. Your mother told me, Etienne, that she imagined you two would want the wedding to be very small, only family perhaps. (Etienne and I exchanged looks of amazement. *Maman* had guessed!) So it will not be long until August for you.

I am writing to ask what you would think about my parents giving a fete the next day here at our house for the friends and neighbors who would like to offer you their good wishes? It would give them a chance to meet Minette, Etienne. You cannot expect to keep her all to yourself forever, you know.

Please think this over and let me know your wishes. My parents send their congratulations to you both. I have been seeing quite a lot of Pierre recently. Isn't it funny how someone you have known all of your life can suddenly appear to you in a new light? I guess we knew each other years and years, and never really saw each other!

Your friend,
Agnes Roussilon

"What a busybody Agnes is," Etienne said, shaking his head.

"Wait Etienne, do not be so hasty. If only our families are present for the wedding, surely it is a good idea to have a fete the following day to meet friends and neighbors. I'd like to meet your friends."

"Maybe you are right," Etienne reluctantly agreed. "I tend to see a red flag whenever Agnes speaks. Her idea is a good one. Will you write to her?"

I knew Etienne shrank from writing even the briefest of notes to Agnes, and while I didn't know whether my writing skills would be equal to the task, I answered that I would gladly write to her. Then, remembering Vincent and the wonderful letters he wrote to me, I knew I could measure up. He had given me confidence in my own abilities.

So I wrote to Agnes, telling her we both were pleased at her suggestion of the fete, spilling out my hopes for a simple summer wedding, telling her of my dream of something light and airy and not at all fussy to wear.

Agnes responded immediately, enclosing clippings from a fashion book with several pictures of lovely summer gowns. One of the pictures was just the sort of dress I'd been longing for. It was all white, a cotton dotted-Swiss fabric with tiny white dots on white. The neck was sweetheart-shaped, edged in a band of very narrow lace. The waist was tied with a grosgrain sash of the palest rose. The sleeves were puffed and ended at the elbow. I thought it was perfect.

I showed the picture to Aunt Titi and Colette and they agreed. Perfect. Days then took on a bustling aspect. First however, the fabric had to be ordered from Paris by the shop on the corner as well as the pale rose grosgrain in just the right width. Then the whir of Aunt Titi's treadle sewing machine could be heard upstairs, after the diners had departed from the cafe. Aunt disdained the idea of ordering any pattern.

"I could make that design with my eyes closed," she said confidently. "Such simplicity, but it is very smart, Minette."

Colette searched through a hundred packets of lace at the thread merchant's shop until she found just the right one to edge the neckline. She asked a lot of questions about Agnes. I could tell she was curious about her, and wanted to know what she looked like. What about her appearance? Was she friendly? Polite but distant? Jealous of you over Etienne? Her questions sounded a litany as we hemmed and stitched. Aunt would allow no machine stitching to show on the outer side of the dress, so there was plenty of hand stitching to be done.

I could tell by the whispers and secret signs when Edith came to the cafe that she and Colette were planning something for me. Then I noticed one day that my best chemise was missing from its place on the shelf of our *armoire*. I said nothing, and in a couple of days it reappeared. So they were making a chemise for me!

In the midst of this flurry of preparations by the womenfolk, Etienne departed, as though anxious to get to his farm and work on his olives and vines, away from such frivolous pursuits. But how I missed him. In Etienne, I realized I had found a true soulmate. When he was away from me, I felt as though a vital part of me was missing. He had promised to come back at least one weekend before the wedding. His letters were full of surprises. He told me about work on the *mas* in greatest detail, describing the peeling walls and the beautiful old doors with equal precision. He described the view of the beautiful old orchard from the windows.

* * *

Aunt had already left for mass at Saint Trophime when I was surprised by a knock on the door one Sunday morning. In summers, the cafe was always closed on Sunday. Colette was still sleeping so I had to hurry down to answer it.

Vincent! There he was standing at the door, wearing his new suit, looking very well trimmed and brushed, looking I thought, a little like a school teacher or . . . a minister! The thought surprised me as I rushed to embrace him.

"Vincent! How wonderful to see you! Is it really you? What on earth are you doing here?" As I rushed to him, I looked over his shoulder and noticed the small man wearing a black suit standing several steps behind, his beetle eyes missing nothing as Vincent and I greeted each other. He had the smallest of feet, encased in patent shoes of a shiny beetle black. Who was he?

"Ah, Minette, one need not fear a cool welcome from you," Vincent said lightly as he stepped back to include the man. "This is Monsieur Trabuc, the chief attendant from Saint Paul de Mausole. We have come down by railway carriage to collect my pictures from your attic, and to see you, Colette and Madame Ginoux of course."

I shook hands with Monsieur Trabuc and welcomed them in, providing coffee and a newspaper for Monsieur Trabuc in the back garden so he could smoke his pipe. Vincent and I sat at a table in the deserted cafe.

"Tell me how you are, Vincent." His paint-stained hands lay folded on the table, his face calm.

"I live from day to day, Minette, but for six months now, since January, I have lived soberly and frugally and healthily. In the past I drank too much alcohol . . . not anymore. In fact, Minette, I am the picture of sobriety now, so much that I think I will start painting in gray."

"You are joking, Vincent!"

"On the contrary, I am dead serious. The bright colors of my Arles days do not seem suited to me in Saint Remy."

I smiled at this, but Vincent quickly reaffirmed his intentions. He was determined to paint in grays. There were eight remaining paintings which he had come to collect. He told me he had been offered a place at the asylum to store his furniture by Dr. Peyron, the physician in charge. He asked me to tell Aunt Titi that someone would call to collect the furniture soon.

I took Vincent up to the attic to retrieve his canvases. He was so glad to see them, handling them lovingly as a father might touch a baby. He was especially pleased to see the view of the orchard he had painted on the day we picnicked with Etienne.

"It needs some reworking," Vincent said. "When I have found the way to express harmony of tones more strongly, I will make another copy of it and send it to you both for my wedding gift."

"Nothing in this world would please us so much," I said, then asked him if he might possibly be able to come to Nimes for our wedding. "It will be quite small, only members of the family. You are like a brother to me, Vincent, I am closer to you than I am to my own brothers. I would like you to be present."

Vincent's eyes took on a faraway look. "Much as I would wish to see you marry, Minnette, I cannot risk it. I talked recently with Dr. Peyron about my condition. He feels, as do I, that I must wait a year before considering myself cured, since the least little thing could bring on another attack. Therefore I must avoid all excitement." He paused.

"Last month I took one walk on the streets of Saint Remy and the sight and noise of such activity upset me terribly. Now, when I go outside the asylum to paint, I go to the silent fields. Nature soothes me, Minette."

Then Vincent told me Theo and his wife were expecting a child. They were also hoping he would be cured soon and would return to Paris.

"But in my heart I know that cannot be," Vincent sadly shook his head. "I must be patient, Minette, and hope that my time spent in Saint Remy will work a cure for me." I wondered if subconsciously Vincent worried the new baby would present another powerful claim on Theo's affections.

However Vincent seemed genuinely fond of Jo, the new sister-in-law, who wrote him enthusiastic letters and seemed to care deeply about him and his work, even though they had not yet met one another.

Vincent said he had hoped to see the Reverend Salles and Dr. Rey at the hospital on this trip, but that he discovered both were away on holiday. "Frankly, I am relieved now, Minette," he said. "I find people tire me."

We returned downstairs to the cafe to find a sleepy Colette trying to come to terms with the morning. She had made a quick *toilette*, and her face was still flushed from sleep.

"What tramping over my head, you two!" she said casually, as though having Vincent in the cafe was the most natural thing in the world. "You sounded like a pair of dancing bears above me. Vincent, how happy I am to see you!" She took both of Vincent's hands and kissed him on both cheeks. Then she excused herself and disappeared in the direction of the kitchen, promising food.

Vincent told me he was reading the works of William Shakespeare, the English playwright.

"Minette, the history plays are marvelous, *Richard II, Henry*

IV and *Henry V.* You must read Shakespeare next, Minette. He is the king of playwrights. His works are immortal."

And so we talked about books, and Etienne, Vincent's paintings, and the artists he loved so much—Millet, Monticelli, Pissarro and others.

Colette appeared with an enormous tray followed by the diminutive Trabuc also staggering under the weight of a laden tray. Soon the four of us were eating a platter of fluffy omelets, toasted bread and honey, and drinking steaming coffee laced with hot milk.

It was a jolly *dejuner* with the solemn-faced Trabuc keeping us laughing with his wry wit. When it was time for them to go, Vincent shook our hands, kissed us both on the forehead, picked up his canvases and walked out of our lives. I wondered when we would see him again.

*   *   *

Edmond and Hubert had been visiting their parents in Avignon the past week and Colette's social life suffered a slump.

"There's no one else around worth walking with," she pouted as we strolled together toward the arena in the cool of evening.

It was a night like Vincent's painting, Stars over the Rhone, with whirling stars like Catherine wheels blazing like a queen's tiara on a carpet of blue black-sky. Lights along the banks of the river gleamed across the water like curling strands of golden hair. Vincent had taught me to see the world differently. He showed me how to find other colors in black skies, colors like blue and purple, rose and yellow. We walked on a bit, not speaking, and I thought of Etienne, wondering if he too might be looking at the same stars.

"I am in a quandary, Minette. I do not know what to do." The strain sounded in Colette's voice.

Quickly my thoughts rushed backward, to the Gauguin

episode. Was Colette in any trouble? "Whatever do you mean?" I took her arm.

"I've been walking out with Edmond and Hubert since almost the first night I was in Arles. They have been great friends. We laugh, we joke, nothing is very serious. Now something has happened and I am afraid."

"What on earth do you mean?"

"I've fallen in love and I don't know what to do."

"Love? Who is it?" My thoughts again flew to Gauguin. Surely he had not been writing to her.

"It is Edmond. I have fallen in love with Edmond, and I do not wish to hurt Hubert." I sighed with relief. Surely this was not an insurmountable problem.

"You silly goose! I thought something terrible had happened, like you had fallen in love with the Prefect, or Monsieur Raspail."

Colette hooted with laughter at the thought of the dour, colorless Prefect and the volatile-tempered cook.

"Be serious, Minette. Don't you see? Hubert has been so kind to me. I cannot hurt his feelings." She did indeed look stricken.

"Pooh, men's hearts mend easily. They are only afraid of losing face, or worse yet, being humiliated. Let me think." We had reached the arena and turned to walk back to the cafe. I was still spellbound by the magic of those stars, all in various colors, as Vincent had showed me, not just white.

"If I were you, Colette, I would confide in Hubert. Confess your feelings for Edmond. By being forthright with him, he will be able to salvage his pride. Maybe he will even gently propel Edmond in your direction." This suggestion seemed logical to my sister.

CHAPTER TWENTY ONE

A letter came from my mother on the sixteenth of July. In it she reiterated her joy at my approaching wedding. She was pleased that only family members would be present and told me that she had sewed a new dress for the occasion. Of course she was still wearing black for my father and Francine, but the neck had a fine lace collar of dark cream. My brothers were pleased to have new suits, the first ones they had ever owned.

"We want you to be proud of your family," she wrote and quickly my eyes filled with tears. I was fiercely proud of them, each and every one. In the closing paragraph she told of startling news.

"Earlier in this day I recalled that I had not paid a visit to Monsieur Van Gogh as I promised you I would," she wrote, "so I took Paul and we made our way to the asylum in mid-afternoon. At the reception desk when I asked to see Monsieur Van Gogh I was told that just last night he suffered another attack and was unable to have visitors. There was nothing else for it but to return home.

"I left a note with the bouquet of roses I had brought to him. I do hope he recovers quickly, but Minette, that place frightens me, I don't mind telling you. The nun in charge seemed positively made of stone, but as we were leaving, a little sister came up to us and whispered not to worry, that the patient was receiving the best care possible. I think she mistook me for a relative."

I pondered this disturbing news, hoping Vincent would recover quickly. But I knew he would be discouraged after going so long without an attack. He must be agonizing on whether or not he could expect these debilitating arracks to occur the rest of his life.

*   *   *

It was in late August, just one week before our wedding, when Etienne had come to Arles for a quick visit, that we at last received a letter from Vincent, confirming the news my mother had written on July sixteenth. He wrote:

Dear Minette and Etienne,

This attack came on me in the fields when I was busy painting . . . on a windy day. I finished in spite of it. It is a painting of the entrance to a quarry, all done in broken greens and reds and rusty yellow ocher. Sometimes I feel a great need to paint using the colors of my native land in the North. I suppose in a way I am homesick for the northern landscape, I know it so well.

For many, many days, almost five weeks, my mind has been absolutely wandering, as it did in Arles, quite as much if not worse, and presumably the attacks will come back in the future. It is abominable.

I am confined to my room and for the last four days I have had a swollen throat and cannot eat. My mental and physical state are considerably weakened and I continue to have the disturbing dreams.

All of this is enough, but worse still, they have taken away my brushes and paints and I am not able to work. This I must admit drives me to the brink of despair. Now I have a promise from the man in charge that if I am able to have a good night's rest, without the nightmares, they will give me my brushes and paints tomorrow.

If this happens I will work on something I can see outside my window, a field of yellow stubble they are ploughing, the contrast of the violet-tinted ploughed earth with the strip of yellow stubble should be quite pleasant. There are hills in the background.

Don't worry when you read this letter as I will probably feeling a lot better by the time you receive it. It's just that I feared you would worry if you did not hear from me and wonder why I have not written. I cannot be other than truthful when I write to tell you why, now can I? I know your wedding must be very soon. My thoughts will be with you. I send my love to you both.

Vincent

"How can they do this to him? Don't they realize that to Vincent, his painting is his life? I knew going to that horrible place would be bad for Vincent!" Furious, I turned to Etienne. This letter was the most agonizing one we had ever received from him.

"Wait, Minette. Think! Why do you suppose they are afraid to give Vincent the painting materials? Think what he has done in past attacks."

As the realization dawned, I saw all too clearly what Etienne was suggesting. Vincent could not be trusted with paint and turpentine. He had swallowed them when the attacks came on before. The doctor was forced to wait until he was sure the attack was over and Vincent had returned to his senses.

I was quite low for a few days, thinking of the disillusionment and despair Vincent must be suffering. How hard he was fighting to keep on painting! Then Etienne received another brief, encouraging note from him, stating that he was definitely improving and had begun to paint. He urged us to give ourselves over to the joy of our coming marriage. We were not to worry about him, he was becoming more and more like himself every day. And he had at last began painting a copy of the Orchard in Spring for us.

*   *   *

What can I say about my wedding other than for me and Etienne, it was the most important wedding in the world. It also presented an opportunity for our families to rejoice with us.

Etienne took the greatest pride in showing my mother and brothers his own land. He showed them the vines, which they were particularly interested to see as the soil around Saint Remy is not suited for vineyards. He took them through the old *mas* which would one day be our home. Already he had begun to replace the broken tiles of the roof and hoped to tile the floors next.

Aunt Titi and my mother established a quick rapport with *Maman Martin*, as she wished to be called. They exchanged several recipes. She especially warmed to my mother because of her double loss of a husband and a child. She saw her as a heroic figure who had kept her family together under very difficult circumstances. And she did everything in her power to make us feel welcome and comfortable.

Colette realized her wish to meet Agnes Roussilon the day after the wedding when we all went to the Roussilons for the fete, so that friends and neighbors could meet Etienne's new bride. With her youth, dark coloring and vigorous health, Colette was a contrast to the fragile-looking Agnes whose beauty was of a delicate type.

Was Agnes's pink beruffled dress of the finest silk just a tiny bit child-like for someone a couple of years older than I? Frankly I thought so, but I said nothing of course. Colette wore the same blouse and skirt in which Vincent painted her and captured many admirers. Even Pierre could not keep from casting glances her way.

But Colette kept her eyes modestly downcast. Since her confession to me of her love for Edmond, she seemed much more introspective and subdued.

Aunt Titi had prepared herself for my departure. She began interviewing replacements for me several weeks earlier, but I was sure she knew nothing of Colette's love for Edmond. But a wedding for Colette and Edmond surely would take place some time in the future. And of course, Edith's baby was due in a month, and her work time at the cafe would be ending.

Instead of preparing a place in her home for Etienne and me, *Maman* decided we should live in the *cabane* occupied by Pierre at present. This would give us a little more room, and a lot more privacy, until the time came when we could move into our own place. I do not know what Pierre thought of this arrangement, but he cheerfully followed his mother's wishes and helped us move in. He in turn moved into one of the rooms of the big house. I was so grateful for the extra room and the privacy.

There was a tiny stove and a sink in the two-room *cabane*. We could have our breakfasts together there, and our suppers. Noontime we joined them at the *mas*. I was still a little in awe of Etienne's mother, so tiny, and such a strong, capable figure. But as time went by I relaxed more in her presence, and we became friends.

There were wedding presents to be stored away until the time when we were in our home. Vincent's painting of the Orchard in Bloom arrived in September at Cafe Ginoux and Aunt Titi sent it on to us in Nimes, along with a letter from Vincent.

Dear Minette and Etienne,

With this letter I send you the copy I promised of the Orchard in Bloom as a token of my deepest affection to you both and as a memento of a happy afternoon spent together in the orchard last spring.

I have been working non-stop since recovering from my attack of last July, eating enough food for two people

and feeling on the whole quite myself again. I have been
working on more versions of the summer wheatfield with
cypresses and have begun a series of painted copies of Labors
of the Field, a series of black and white woodcuts after Millet.
You remember Monsieur Trabuc, Minette, from my most
recent visit? Well, I have finished a portrait of him which I
started working on early in September.

In some ways he looks stern with his black eyes, like a
bird of prey, but his face has been softened by years of
service to the suffering. M. Trabuc has the features of the
People, by that I mean he is one of the legions of hard-
working souls who keep this world turning by doing the
dirty jobs not many are willing to perform. He is a worker.
As I have not been away from my room in the past two
months, I have seen a lot of Trabuc. He has been my only
contact with a world of sanity for all practical purposes. In
this portrait, I have tried to give a view of the inner man
through his appearance in which a contemplative calm comes
through most strongly. I plan to paint his wife's portrait in a
few days.

Soon I hope to be going out of doors to paint. I have
been studying the olive trees around here and feel they
would offer great substance and symbolism in a series of
paintings I am eager to begin!

I hope to visit Arles again soon and pay a visit to good
Madame Ginoux, whom I missed on my last visit. I know
she and Colette will furnish me with all the details of your
wedding. Perhaps someday I too will join that rarefied group
of happily married couples! Word from my brother and his
wife that when the new baby arrives, he will be called
Vincent, for me. A bit of myself for posterity, eh?

A serious word to close: Dr. Peyron, the head of the
asylum has told me and my brother whom he visited while
in Paris recently, that he does not believe I am mad. He
believes I am perfectly sane and that the attacks are brought

on by a form of epilepsy. This news makes me feel better in one way, but oh how I dread the onset of another attack which I suppose is inevitable. I am beginning to think my constitution is not made for this climate and that perhaps my health would strengthen if I returned to my native North.

I think of you both, my favorite friends of the Midi, joined together in matrimony, and my heart is gladdened.

Yours,
Vincent

Poor, poor Vincent, I thought as Etienne and I sat comfortably together in the little *cabane*, lighted by a flickering candle. Supper was over. It was the quiet, private time we had each day to share our thoughts before an early bedtime. Etienne liked to be working as soon after daybreak as possible.

"He does not say anything in the letter about how long he will remain in Saint Remy," I said.

"And this is the first time I have heard him say he is thinking about a return to the North," Etienne mused. "I wonder how his family feels about that?"

"He said when he left Arles he would stay in the asylum for a year. It looks like he feels his time there has lasted long enough."

"Especially as they seem to be doing nothing to treat his illness. It is a case of letting the attacks run their course when they occur," Etienne said, putting aside the letter. What neither of us knew for certain then was that Vincent's days in the Midi were drawing to a close. Increasingly he thought about the North and longed to be there painting once more. His people were there, and he was beginning to feel the climate and geography were more congenial to his temperament.

The painting which was his gift to us was to my mind one of the most beautiful he ever painted. Part of its beauty for me derived from the memory of a happy day the three of us shared together. It was my memento of Vincent, of Arles, and of Etienne and myself in the days of our courtship.

I missed Arles. I had been very happy there with the bustle of the cafe, the kind supervision of my aunt, my establishing a close relationship with my sister Colette. Although I did not speak of this to Etienne, he wisely realized I was homesick for my family, so in late October he planned a weekend visit to Arles and Saint Remy.

I began counting the days until our departure.

*   *   *

Colette wrote to us that Aunt had at last hired a new girl as waitress, the niece of Monsieur Raspail, the cook. She came from Marseilles. "She carries the orders out from the kitchen with the speed of lightening, but she is eating me out of house and home," Aunt Titi fussed. The new girl, Joan, liked to eat before and after she served. "Just a taste, you understand," she said to my aunt. But she was efficient and took over a lot of the work Aunt Titi had been doing since my departure.

As to her appearance, Colette took few words to describe her: "Twentyish, black hair in a bun, many bracelets and plump, plump, plump." The washing of the cafe linens had reverted back to the laundress, as Colette was too busy to undertake it alone. Besides, she said, our mother had written her that she was getting our farm back into a profit at last. "Everyone can breathe easier now," she wrote.

The most surprising news in her letter concerned Hubert. When he and Edmond returned from Avignon to visit their parents, Hubert began to invite Suzette, the baker's assistant, to walk out with him. The same girl Etienne had taken for walks a few times before he and I became betrothed. I wrote Colette asking for more of an explanation.

She replied, "I found a moment alone with Hubert on the first night they returned from Avignon. I told him of my feelings for

Edmond as you suggested. Hubert said he understood. Since then he's been walking with Suzette. Edmond comes here to walk with me, but he hasn't said anything yet about caring for me in any special way. I hope I haven't made a blunder, Minette. I would be miserable if I lost Edmond." I thought my advice had been logical. Surely Edmond would now speak up!

As for Vincent, his letters were episodic, not, I think because he wished it, but because of his health. There were times when his mental state was simply too fragile to perform the task of collecting his thoughts and setting them down in a letter. Once he fully recovered from an attack, however, he quickly resumed the letter writing.

He was receiving fewer letters from Theo, and this was a worry, he wrote. Theo, now responsible for a wife and an unborn child, also had his job at the art gallery plus the support of a brother and the artist Gauguin, who still received a monthly stipend.

Gauguin was now as far away from Vincent as he could manage, I thought bitterly, working in Brittany.

In one of his letters, written to Etienne and me in early October, Vincent wrote, "I am feeling well just now. I think Dr. Peyron is right when he says I am not strictly speaking mad, for my mind is absolutely normal in the intervals between attacks, even more so than before." (He had written this earlier; it must be heavy on his mind.) "But during the attacks, it is terrible, and I lose consciousness of everything. But that spurs me on to my work and to seriousness, like a miner who is always in danger makes haste in what he does."

Poor Vincent. My heart broke for him when I read those words. Was he remembering his stay in the coal mining district of Belgium, the Borinage? He had gone down into the mines then with the miners in order to understand them better as their minister.

He wrote that he was now using the motif of the olive trees which were so abundant around Saint Remy. "I want so much to capture the essence of them," he said. "Silver against a soil of orange and violet hues, under the large white sun of the coming winter. I believe it is something no other painter has done." I found it amazing that he could time and time again throw himself so energetically into his work after such devastating setbacks. Vincent's letters were always frank and forthright. He went on to say he was running out of paints and wondering why he had no word from his brother in over twenty days. Yet at the same time he spoke of Theo's many responsibilities and worries. Vincent's mother and his sister, Wil, were also a concern for Theo, even though they were financially independent of him.

"So when I have no paints, instead of painting, I take long walks, studying the effects of autumn on the countryside around Saint Remy. I miss the Arles vineyards, so lovely this time of year, but as you know Minette, there are hardly any grapes grown in this area. The soil is not right."

"Minette," the letter continued, "I have recently recalled an event of last June, around June sixteenth. The memory of it had completely left me, I only remembered today when I came across a sketch I had made sometime after, a drawing of a beautiful bouquet of pale pink roses. I made the sketch following an attack, and when I asked at the time where the roses came from, I was told they had been brought to me by a Madame Ginoux and her son Paul.

"Minette, tell your mother and brother how deep is my regret not to have acknowledged this kindness. The drawing is one of my best. The roses are arranged in a terra cotta vase with a background of a yellow-green wall and a darker green cloth covering the table on which they stand. When Theo sends me paints, I plan to make several copies in oils. Please convey to your mother my sincere thanks for her thoughtfulness, and my apology for my tardy response."

Etienne decided then and there after finishing Vincent's letter that we would call upon Vincent on the weekend when we were visiting Aunt Titi in Arles and my mother in Saint Remy, although I dreaded going to Saint Paul de Mausole, the asylum.

*   *   *

Early in September Etienne asked me if I would like to take over the *lavandin* plot on the farm. Lavender oil was a profitable crop in Provence. I could take the lavender to the oil producers, who would pay well for good lavender. Etienne told me I could use the money earned to buy things for the *mas* which I especially wanted.

If the venture succeeded, I might try making lavender bags with part of the crop and then sell them at the herb market in Avignon, where I had heard prices paid were higher than at Nimes.

Many of the plants I discovered were very old and had to be cut back severely in order to produce healthy new growth. I took the clippings and planted new rows of cuttings, but because it was late in the season I would have to protect them from the cold in winter and might lose them. Next year, I would take the cuttings earlier.

There were so many things I wished for! Gingham for the curtains at the windows, a large round table and ladderback chairs for the big room near the kitchen where we would spend most of our time, a bed with a carved headboard, a chest carved with Biblical scenes, similar to *Maman's* chest.

"Stop, Minette," Etienne laughed as I reeled off the list. "You are growing *lavandin,* not gold coins." It was after our supper, and we were sitting in the *cabane* before going to bed.

Etienne too had dreams. He dreamed of a larger winepress so we could bottle our own wine in greater quantity and sell it at the market, fine cattle and a few chickens, and most of all, he wanted new nursery stock—peaches and apricots—to renew the old orchard on the property.

*   *   *

Etienne and I had our first real quarrel the night before we planned to leave for Arles. That night the *mistral* wind came up.

When it began to blow Etienne declared that he would not be able to leave the following day to make the trip. The winds would damage the new roof tiles unless they were carefully secured. It meant I would have to go on without him. If he was able to get the roof tiles secured, he would join me the following day in Saint Remy and we could visit Vincent together. Meanwhile, I was to go on *the diligence,* the stagecoach, the next morning as we had planned.

This turn of events upset me terribly. I wanted to make my first reappearance in Arles and Saint Remy with my new husband. And the thought of going to Saint Paul de Mausole alone to see Vincent filled me with an unreasonable terror.

"Please, Etienne," I begged. "Do not let me go alone. Think of how everyone will be expecting us both." Stony-faced he regarded me, the green eyes taking on lambent flashes. His body sagged with fatigue on the couch where we sat at opposite ends. He had been working terribly hard.

"You need a rest, Etienne. Come, let us go together as we planned," I coaxed. He shook his head and said nothing.

This was the agreeable, even-tempered man I had married. So willing and so easy to please. But with a stubbornness the size of the Alpilles mountain range. I discovered that night one thing meant as much to Etienne as I did—he cared the world for his land. The blood of generations of Provencal farmers coursed energetically through his veins. He was a captive to the land as though iron chains bound him to it, and he would not give in.

Hurt and angry I prepared for bed. I realized that nothing I could do would change his mind. If I made the trip, I would have to go alone. As he climbed into the bed beside me I turned away pretending sleep. My heart was heavy because it was our first quarrel, and we were both angry as we went to sleep. But both of us were too proud to give in.

The next morning as I prepared to leave we were still silent. I think we learned something about each other because of that quarrel. Both of us could be unreasonably stubborn.

Etienne stood stiffly at my side as we waited in the square at Nimes for the arrival of the *diligence*. The journey by stagecoach, though more expensive, was by far quicker than a chance ride on a farm wagon. As the *diligence* entered the square, Etienne quickly gathered me in his arms and whispered, "Go safely, *cherie*. I will be only half-alive until we are together again."

I clung to him, ashamed of the tears that rolled down my cheeks. Then I climbed up into the stagecoach and settled into the seat next to a lady. I looked at Etienne until he was only a tiny figure as the *diligence* rumbled toward Arles.

CHAPTER TWENTY TWO

The plane trees lining the road leading to Saint Paul de Mausole had lost their leaves and the skeletal shapes of the bleached white branches seemed to reach out to me as I walked. Etienne and I had written to Vincent from Nimes, asking to visit him on the Sunday afternoon when we would be spending the day in Saint Remy. That was before Etienne elected to stay in Nimes and ride out the *mistral* as it hammered away at the roof he had been rebuilding. I was alone as I approached the asylum and I wished with all my heart Etienne could be with me. My mother, suffering from *grippe*, was unable to accompany me. I could not ask my brothers because I knew they had planned to work in the fields that afternoon.

Vincent had replied to our letter, saying that his recovery from the most recent attack had been very slow. He was still somewhat agitated, but had received permission to welcome us on the Sunday. He suggested our meeting take place in the gardens, as there was more privacy there.

The *mistral* winds had died down by the time I left Arles for Saint Remy. The visit with Aunt Titi and Colette had seemed somewhat strange, as they were busy in their work, and I was no longer a part of it. I didn't feel the same about the cafe at Arles, although the welcome my aunt and my sister gave me was warm and loving. I kept thinking of Etienne and the farm, wondering what he was doing at particular moments, hoping he would be thinking of me, regretting our stupid quarrel.

It was the same when I arrived at my mother's house in Saint Remy. My life there, while rich in memory, was a thing of the past. I had new duties and responsibilities now, I reminded myself, and yes, new interests. Even Francine, whom I had loved so dearly, had receded into a niche of the past to which I would never return, no matter how often I visited Saint Remy. My mother and I found it was too soon for us to talk about Francine. "Later," she said firmly, "When our grief has healed a little."

And so I walked thoughtfully along the gloomy path, toward the meeting with Vincent, wishing with every step that Etienne could be by my side. Inside the building I confronted the sister at the reception desk who peered suspiciously out at me from behind the thick lenses of her spectacles.

I thought she looked at me disapprovingly as she inquired, "You are Madame Martin? Your husband is also expected?"

"He has been delayed by an emergency," I replied. Then, as an afterthought, "I expect him to join me." I added that because she looked so stern and I was afraid of not being able to see Vincent after traveling so far. It would be such an act of cruelty to keep us from meeting, I thought.

I straightened my back and stood tall, looking her in the eye.

"Sister Theresa," she lowered her gaze, turned, and called to a young novice standing beside the door, "Take Madame Martin to the garden." I breathed a sigh of relief.

Like the institution of Saint Paul de Mausole, the garden seemed to be on its last legs, a desolate place in winter, giving the impression of having known better times. There were neglected flower beds, taken over by rampaging ivy, the tendrils giving a soft patina to the tree trunks on which it twined. Nothing of course was in bloom at this time of year. I wondered what it looked like in spring. The young novice left me, the wide wings of her headdress flopping, borne aloft by the wind as she walked.

Then I saw Vincent striding toward me, a folio under his arm. I had a moment to take in his appearance before we greeted each other. He was wearing a blue coat and darker blue trousers. He was clean shaven and looked neat. His hair was cut short. I was struck by how physically well he looked. His color was ruddy, he seemed strong and well-fed. His steps were sure. Only looking into his eyes and at his mouth did I detect a change. The intensity of the blue pupils was the same, but I sensed resignation there. Vincent's eyes told me he had accepted his condition as inevitable. The firm set of his mouth was new and told me that while resigned to his fate, he also was in complete control.

We shook hands and he kissed me on both cheeks. I was certain that from within the somber walls of the asylum we were being watched, if not by the inmates, then by the cold, distant nuns.

"So you came! Where is Etienne?" Quickly I explained about the *mistral* in a bantering voice. Vincent laughed.

"Minette, Minette, so early in your marriage and you already have a rival! Etienne will make a fine farmer. His land is close to his heart, almost as close as you are!" He smiled and I relaxed. He seemed exactly like the genial, easygoing Vincent I remembered.

"You look well, Vincent. I worried on my journey that you might be too fatigued to see me."

He passed a hand over his eyes. "I recover. My will is strong. But there seems always to be another demon lurking around the corner to tease me. I cannot seem to escape the fact, Minette. I heard from my brother today. He is making inquiries on my behalf to locate a place for me near Paris. He thinks he may have found it at Auvers-sur-Oise, a small village north of Paris. There is a doctor there who is also an artist of sorts, an amateur, you understand. Theo believes, as does an artist friend of ours, Pissarro, that this man may help me. Gachet is his name."

"But Vincent, surely you do not mean to leave Provence!" My voice quavered. "You have done such marvelous work in Arles,

Vincent. The harvests, the sunflowers, the orchards—they all cry out to be painted by you."

"It is so good to be in your company, Minette. I have always known it. But listen, I will be honest with you, the climate in Provence affects me in a disastrous way. The *mistral* winds. the storms, I feel it is so foreign from what I have known. It must be causing this disharmony within me." There was a desperation in his voice I'd never heard before.

We sat for a few minutes on the bench not speaking as a great feeling of sadness filled my heart. I had supposed Vincent would return to Arles when his time at Saint Remy was finished. Had Arles become an unhappy memory for Vincent? The Little Yellow House no longer was his haven; Gauguin, the evil man, had left him. Postmaster Roulin and his family had moved to Marseilles and Etienne and I to Nimes. True, Colette and Aunt Titi were still there, but it was not the same. And then there was the unspeakable ugliness of Vincent's neighbors who had circulated the petition. I could understand how Vincent felt.

"Tell me about your painting, Vincent," I said, hoping to bring our visit around to happier thoughts.

"Ah, yes," he began, "The one constant in my life is my work. Remember Minette, there will be flowers and harvests and orchards and trees wherever I go. And I will paint them. There is another possibility, Minette, that I might go to Brittany for a month to paint with Gauguin. Did you know we have been writing to each other? I have mentioned to him that I would be glad to come to Brittany to work with him again, but as yet I have had no reply."

The possibility of Gauguin extending such an invitation to Vincent was as likely as snow falling in July, I thought scornfully, but I said nothing. Vincent had a blind spot where Gauguin was concerned. He was incapable of seeing the many faults of the man.

As though reading my thoughts Vincent took my hand and said, "Your face is an open book, Minette. I can tell what your feelings are about Gauguin just by looking at you. You do not need to open your mouth! Your feelings about him are right in so many ways. I know it. But listen, his instruction to me in Arles was invaluable to my painting.

"In my time here," he motioned toward the asylum building, "I have been unable to find congenial companionship, much less instruction. There are no models. Can you imagine trying to paint these poor souls who are little better than the walking dead?"

He continued, "When I was weak and disoriented after an attack, I could not venture out into the world to paint. This is where the value of Gauguin's teaching saved me. He is the one who told me time after time, 'It is all in your head, Vincent. Paint from your imagination.' And it saved me." He stroked his chin in thought.

"I have been able to work on every day save at the worst times. So maybe he does things which you do not like, Minette, I do not deny it. But if he has been a redeeming influence on just one person, me, and my work, is it not worthwhile?"

I sat there pondering Vincent's words. I could not be so generous toward Gauguin as he, but I turned to him after murmuring, "Perhaps you are right, Vincent. Let me see some of your work now." His face lit up. It was clear he still saw his life as a mission— a mission to keep painting as much as he possibly could.

First he showed me a frieze-like close-up of life size irises, painted within the first week of his arrival. One lone white iris blossom stood out like a giant butterfly. Each delicate flower head, each sword-like frond was rendered powerfully with bursting life and vitality. The closeness to the image suggested to me a microcosm of the entire species. I thought it was one of the most beautiful oil paintings I had ever seen, and I told him so. His eyes took on the deep blue fire I remembered, and I knew he was pleased.

There were other garden paintings, an oil of the trees of the garden and the very bench we were seated on. The ground and the tree trunks were spangled with ivy. There were brown ink drawings done with a reed pen. There was one of a deserted garden done in pen and colored chalk. There were drawings of black ink and gouache of the vestibule and corridor of Saint Paul de Mausole.

"Why are there no people in these, Vincent?" I asked.

"There are very few people here, Minette," he answered. "In the men's wing alone, there are thirty vacant rooms." So this accounted for the run down appearance of everything, I thought. What a depressing place for Vincent!

"Another reason is that there aren't any desirable models to put in the pictures. I won't inhabit my pictures with madmen!" he said suddenly, with great feeling. I realized how painfully difficult his life must be.

"But we are lucky in one way, Minette. The poor souls never visit the garden. I thought we could avoid all of the disharmony and ugliness by meeting here."

Next Vincent showed me a series of paintings of the fields. One a field of blooming poppies, another with the background of the rounded Alpilles under a vibrant sky. A golden wheat field in the center of which rose the dark, upward curving branches of a cypress tree, the tree that is emblematic of Saint Remy and its environs. Yellow roofs of a house in the distance echoed the golden wheat.

Lastly, Vincent brought out a group of paintings of olive trees.

"Where did you find all these wonderful fields, Vincent?" I was unaware that such beauty existed in the area around Saint Remy. The powerful, expressive brush strokes caught my attention.

"A few were views from the windows here. On rare occasions when I felt especially strong, I went out into the fields. But here is one painted entirely from memory." He handed me the one he called Olive Trees with the Alpilles in the Background. The olive tree trunks were convoluted and misshapen with the ground in which they stood rolling and mounded in an exaggerated way. Mountains loomed darkly violet and blue black, alien shapes seeming to take on a life of their own.

In the sky the anthropomorphic outline of a white and yellow cloud hovered, looking for all the world like a shroud-wrapped apparition. To be truthful I found the picture rather disturbing because of the exaggerated shapes of natural things, yet its coloring was spectacularly beautiful.

"This one, Minette, I painted as a textbook example of Gauguin's technique. It is a Brittany landscape painted in the heart of sunny Provence."

I told Vincent I felt his painting skills had not suffered, in spite of his poor health. This pleased him greatly. "It is such a joy to see you and be with you, Minette. How happy I would have been if fate had put us together. But no more of that! You have found your true soulmate. Etienne has a good heart equal to yours. You are meant for each other. You will never know how many times I have thought of the lovely girl with the coffee-tinted skin, on that first night in Arles when she took me in and let me sleep by the embers of the kitchen fire. I will never forget your kindness, Minette."

Somewhat embarrassed, I asked him about his brother and his sister-in-law, Jo.

"Jo is a wonderful girl. She writes me letters about what is going on in the art world in Paris. She knows I am trying to keep abreast of new trends here on this alien planet of Saint Paul de Mausole! I believe becoming a godfather for the baby will be good for me, don't you, Minette? Whether it is a boy or a girl. Did I write you Minette, that if it is a boy, they will call him Vincent?" He looked pleased.

Dusk descended on the garden as shadows lengthened and took on surreal shapes. A decided coolness permeated the air. I rose to go.

"I must hurry, Vincent. My mother will begin to worry as darkness approaches. This chill air cannot be good for you either."

"Theo has sent me a warm woolen vest so I can be comfortable out of doors painting in chilly weather," he answered absently. I could tell he was lost in thoughts which I could not share. I stood up and he took my hands.

"Dear Friend, do not forget me. I will keep you in my thoughts always. Give good Etienne my true regards. We will meet again sometime."

Quickly I turned away before he could see my eyes swimming in tears. The lump in my throat was unbearable. I groped in my pocket for a handkerchief as I walked away. Why did life have to be so sad? Must we lose everything we cherish? There were no answers, I knew, but I turned around anyway, for one last look at Vincent. He had stopped at the stairs. He stood there and raised a hand in salute. Then he turned and walked into the building.

CHAPTER TWENTY THREE

When I returned to the farm I was so glad to see Etienne, so glad to be with him, that all thoughts of being homesick for Arles were banished to the back of my mind. Immediately after supper I sat down with him and began to tell him everything about my visit. I did my best to reconstruct my meeting with Vincent, down to the tiniest detail.

I described the overgrown garden where we met, the weather, the atmosphere of Saint Paul de Mausole from the threatening arms of the bare plane trees to the ivy clamping a stranglehold on everything it touched. I tried to remember every sentence we had spoken. I told him about Vincent's pictures, works he had finished since his arrival in Saint Remy.

Etienne listened to it all very carefully. I waited for him to speak.

"It is odd that he feels the attacks may be brought on by the climate of Provence," he said at last.

"Yes, perhaps he is grasping at straws, but Etienne, they have not come up with any other explanations! Not his diet, not his habits, nothing. The same is true of the hospital doctor of the *Hotel Dieu* in Arles. He failed to discover a cause of the attacks."

"Vincent is an individual in his illness as he is in his art,"

Etienne said wisely. "Maybe Vincent is right. Possibly the Midi is bad for his constitution. I am sorry he wishes to leave."

In my letter to Aunt Titi and Colette I asked them if Vincent had so much as mentioned his possible departure for the North.

"He never spoke of it to me," replied my aunt. "I thought he was planning to return here when his year in Saint Remy was finished. Else why would I be keeping his furniture?"

I puzzled over Vincent's situation as another Advent season approached. I was busy planning our observances, but I took the time to select a new novel by Zola and sent it off to Vincent. And I expected to hear from him any day.

But Vincent's letters were sporadic at best. One brief note to us after our visit together in October. That was all. Then, in February:

Dear Minette and Etienne:

You doubtless have wondered what kind of a friend I am for not being in touch sooner. A few days before Christmas, a year to the day after I suffered my first attack in Arles, I was struck down again. This time I was working perfectly calmly on some canvases when suddenly, without any warning, the aberration seized me.

I rallied in about a week and began to work. These wretched setbacks play havoc with my painting. Then I had a visit from the Reverend Salles from Arles. I was glad to see him as he is one of the few who have stuck with me, including of course you two. Next I was occupied sending a crate of my pictures off to my brother in Paris. Frankly, I do not like to have many pictures lying about. You never know when some of the poor souls here might find them and set them alight. By the way, I told the Reverend Salles, as I have told my brother, that they should never, never recommend this place to anyone.

I have found out about another place, an asylum near Avignon, at Montdevergues. It sounds much better than this place, and is cheaper and the clothing for the patients is furnished. Instead of remaining idle all day, the patients there work in the fields, giving them both physical and mental occupation. There is also a forge, where some of them are employed under the supervision of a blacksmith. Finally, there is a carpenters shop. This would provide one with more active, alert companions and also models for pictures and drawings.

Have you heard of this place? If not, could you find out something about it for me? I know Nimes is close by Avignon, so it cannot be far from you. I would be most grateful.

After this litany of misfortunes, you will be glad to read of some good news. My little namesake, a healthy baby boy, has arrived and is doing well, according to both of his parents. He has a strong voice and cries a lot, but is vigorous and growing rapidly. I have in mind painting branches of almond blossoms seen against a blue sky. The almond trees will be coming into bloom soon. This painting I will give to him as a token of my love.

There is other good news. I think I told you about a group of artists called *Les XX*, the Twenty, in Belgium, who are holding an exhibition in Brussels soon. They have asked to exhibit my work so Theo has promised to send pictures as soon as they are framed. I have chosen Wheat Field with Rising Sun which I believe I showed you, Minette when you were in Saint Remy, and two Artist's Bedroom scenes, variants on the Arles bedroom. Finally, two views of olive trees. Theo assures me they will be framed in time to send off.

I am anxious to hear of the work on your house. Now that the roof tiles are in place, how are you progressing on the floors, Etienne? And when will you put in the new nursery stock for the orchard? I have had no word from Madame Ginoux in Arles. I trust everything is well there.

Grateful but tardy thanks for the new Zola novel which
I have read and reread with much pleasure. You two are
better to me than I deserve. Please write to me about what
you are reading, Minette.

Your Friend,
Vincent

It was a relief to hear of course, but much of the news was
distressing. And no word at all in the letter about returning to the
North. Etienne had heard of the asylum near Avignon, but he had
no specific information. He promised me then and there that we
would drive by to check it out after the next market day in Avignon,
and we would make inquiries that might prove useful to Vincent.

Etienne was as good as his word. The following market day he
borrowed the carriage from *Maman* and we set out early for
Avignon, planning to visit the asylum at Montdevergues on our
way back home.

It was an austere looking place, not nearly so beautiful as the
somber old monastery of Saint Paul de Mausole. What trees there
might have been surrounding the building had been felled and
the ground turned into vegetable fields, where we could see a
number of patients working, all dressed identically in brown
homespun, among the rows of chard and cabbages.

While it was not nearly so picturesque and romantic as Saint
Paul de Mausole, it had an energy about it completely lacking in
Saint Remy with its feeling of lassitude. I saw several figures who
might make attractive models for Vincent to paint.

We pulled up at the forge and were welcomed by the
blacksmith, a jolly looking man with a rounded middle and eyes
which crinkled with good humor. He was supervising half a dozen
men who were busy hammering horseshoes into shape. They were
wearing the same brown homespun as the field workers.

While Etienne questioned the blacksmith, I quietly observed
the patients at work. They seemed engaged in their task and looked

SEEKING THE HIGH YELLOW NOTE

quite normal. Had they been walking the streets of Avignon, I would not have thought them anything but average, normal workingmen. Certainly I would not have thought they were patients in a mental asylum. Maybe this place would be a possibility for Vincent. It would mean we could be in contact with him much more easily.

"So what do you think?" I asked as we started for home in the carriage.

"I think it is possibly a better situation than Vincent has at Saint Remy. The patients who are able to work are certainly better off, if in Saint Remy they only spend their days in idleness as Vincent declares. Of course, we do not know the situation of those unable to work. Nor do we know what sort of treatment is offered there. Vincent has said in all the months at Saint Paul de Mausole, he has never been given any cure or treatment."

"And Vincent could have normal looking people for models in his paintings," I added as Etienne stroked his chin in thought.

"Perhaps," said Etienne. "I will write to him of everything we have seen and heard." And Etienne wrote Vincent a long letter describing in detail our visit.

*   *   *

Colette wrote that Aunt Titi had come down with a sickness and had been forced to take to her bed. Colette, Joan, the other waitress, and Monsieur Raspail, the cook, were managing to carry on, but they had been forced to shorten the cafe menu and to give up, at least temporarily, the homemade pates which my aunt took such pride in making and serving to her patrons.

Colette feared that if she did not improve soon, they might be forced to offer only one meal a day, and "then where would we be?" she wrote. I answered her immediately, asking her to send me word in a few days. Aunt Titi was as close to me as my own mother, in fact, I think she understood me better. Naturally I was worried.

The next word from Colette was very brief. No change in Aunt's condition. After reading her note I threw on my shawl and hurried to the *mas* where Etienne was working on the new floor tiles. I read Colette's brief letter to him.

"You should go at once," he said, and I hurried back to the *cabane* to pack my things. By afternoon I was on the *diligence* bound for Arles, with some restorative syrups and brandy from *Maman* tucked into my basket.

The cafe looked as it always had as I stepped in and a flustered Joan took me at once up to Aunt Titi. I was shocked at the appearance of my beautiful Aunt, the Arlesienne, painted by Vincent. Her face looked white as the pillow on which her head rested, the eyes seemed overbright, a result of the fever I supposed. Her breathing seemed labored.

"Minette," she said in a weak voice. "So you have come."

"I am here Aunt, to see you begin to mend and to help in the cafe." My voice rang out like a trumpet, but I was determined to keep a cheerful tone in the sickroom. I thought at that moment of Vincent and how he always kept his spirits up, even when things were the blackest.

Aunt Titi's eyes flickered and a ghost of a smile crossed her wan face. "It is good to see you, Minette and to know you have come to help." Her eyes fluttered and closed and she slept.

Relief shone in Colette's eyes when she saw me. She had gone to the baker to collect bread when I arrived.

"Thank goodness you are here! I dared not ask you to come, but I prayed that you would. It was all right with Etienne?"

"He suggested it after the second letter arrived. How do you think Aunt is doing?"

"The doctor thinks it is pneumonia. But he cannot understand why the fever lingers on. He is concerned because she has no energy and wants to sleep all of the time."

"I wrote to Saint Remy, both to Vincent and to our family. I thought they should know her condition."

A letter of reply came immediately from Vincent. He expressed his sorrow at "Madame Ginoux's indisposition" and he was hopeful he would be able to call upon her soon to "inquire after her health." He said he would also be glad to see me and "Mademoiselle Colette."

But February slipped into March and we saw nothing of Vincent. Remarkably, the elixir sent by *Maman Martin* seemed to do the trick for Aunt Titi. She regained her strength amazingly soon and was able to leave her bed, although she was not yet able to resume her more strenuous duties.

Joan, Colette and I were managing very well, except that I began having a stomach complaint. At the least feeling of queasiness I would bring up whatever I had eaten. This was accompanied by feelings of nausea. I could hardly make myself go into the steaming kitchen where cooking odors assailed from every side. Those smells were sure to upset me and send me running to the wash room.

It was the height of the noonday lunch. I was serving a pork roast cooked with apples to a table of workmen when my stomach began to turn over dangerously. I set down the platter on which globules of fat from the roast swam in the sauce, and hurried as fast as my feet would take me to the wash room in the corridor. After vomiting, I immediately felt better, but I was worried about the constant nausea.

I told Colette of my discomfort and asked her if she remembered any such complaint of our mother or father. She thought for a minute and said she did not. "Nobody in our family ever had a stomach complaint."

The next time I was forced to run to the wash room, Aunt was waiting for me when I emerged.

"Are you all right? What is the matter?"

"I have been having an upset stomach of late. I do not know what is causing it, but I feel a nausea when I see or worse yet, smell certain foods."

"And these upset stomachs, when do they occur?" She was smiling in a friendly way as she scrutinized my face.

"Usually early in the morning," I answered. "You can't be sure however. Yesterday it was the pork roasted with apples that set me off."

"Ah, I see," said my aunt. "It must have been the rich smell of the meat which set off the queasiness. By the way, have you had your 'normal time' this month?" Her voice was all innocence.

Surprised and embarrassed I looked quickly at her face. What right had she to ask me such personal questions? But, come to think, I was late, no question about that. Blushing furiously as I slowly understood, I shook my head. What a fool I had been. It was no stomach complaint. It was morning sickness. I was pregnant!

"You little goose," whispered my aunt as she embraced me. "That is what is wrong with you. Don't worry, I will keep your secret until you are ready."

*   *   *

The following Sunday I was surprised to see Monsieur Trabuc from Saint Paul de Mausole enter the cafe. Seeing me he hurried to my side and asked if we might speak privately a few moments.

What has happened to Vincent, I thought, flustered, as I led him to the back corridor. What could have happened to him? My heart was drumming. I knew it must be something of a worrying nature.

"Mademoiselle," he began and I did not correct him as he was in an agitated state. After all, he had no reason to know I was now Madame Martin. "I have come to Arles to search for Monsieur Vincent. He has gone missing. He left Saint Remy yesterday by railway, planning to travel to Arles to visit Madame Ginoux. He left carrying a canvas he planned to give to her. He did not return on the evening train." He cleared his throat nervously.

My face went blank. Vincent hadn't been here. There must be some mistake.

"Have you seen him? We are alarmed, we fear he may be ill. Has he been here?"

"No," I answered. "We have seen nothing of him. He wrote a week or so ago saying he was sorry my aunt had been ill and he hoped to call upon her soon."

The look on Trabuc's face was a study in concern. I realized he cared for Vincent and was very worried. "When he did not arrive, we feared another attack had occurred."

"He has been well, and I personally put him on the train myself," Trabuc said, rubbing his chin, the beetle eyes darting back and forth. "He was in good spirits when I put him on the Saturday morning train."

"Have you checked the hospital? He liked to keep in touch with Dr. Rey there." I racked my brain. "Then there is the Reverend Salles, the Protestant minister in Arles. Vincent considered him a friend. Maybe he went to visit there."

"This is the first call I have made," Trabuc admitted, "Since he told me he intended to go to Arles in the first place to call upon Madame Ginoux." Trabuc shook his head.

"I suggest you also go by his former house at Number Two, Place Lamartine. Vincent loved that house. It is possible he wanted to see it again. He may even have spent the night there!"

Where, oh where could Vincent be? Mental pictures of Vincent lying cold in a field alone flashed through my mind as Trabuc left the cafe. He promised to let me know what he discovered.

By mid-afternoon Trabuc returned to the cafe without Vincent. He and the carriage driver had been to the *Hotel Dieu*, but nobody in the hospital, including Dr. Rey, had seen Vincent. The Little Yellow House was deserted, empty, padlocked. No sign of him there. The Reverend Salles was just as puzzled as the rest of us. Nobody, it seems, had seen him.

Trabuc was at his wit's end. His patient seemed to have vanished into thin air. Aunt Titi and Colette joined us, bringing coffee and we sat around one of the cafe tables, wondering where on earth Vincent had gone.

My aunt, although still pale from her recent illness, had dressed as always with great care. She made an immediate conquest of

Monsieur Trabuc who looked at her admiringly. She glanced his way, her beautiful brown eyes wide, and coughed delicately behind a snowy handkerchief.

"Monsieur Trabuc, have you searched the *Maison de Tolerance* in Arles?" Aunt Titi suggesting he search at the brothel! I could not believe it. Colette gave me one of her looks.

Aunt Titi modestly lowered her eyes and waited. Trabuc suddenly was all interest. Here was a suggestion, at last, that might lead to something!

"And what makes you think he might be there, Madame?" His voice was little more than a whisper.

"Because he has been there before," she said it casually, shrugging with great *elan*, as if to say, we two at this table are older, we know the ways of the world.

At once Trabuc was on his tiny feet and speeding toward the door and the waiting carriage like an impatient bloodhound.

"He didn't even have to ask where it was," Colette observed.

"Men know those things," Aunt Titi said, and as usual, she was probably right.

Within the hour Trabuc was knocking on the door again. "We have found him," he announced, "Where you suggested, Madame." He bowed low to her. "He apparently consumed a vast quantity of wine yesterday, fell into a deep sleep and only a short time ago awoke, not knowing where he was or why he was there. By the hardest work I was able to administer a sedative and help him into the carriage. He is asleep there now. We must return to Saint Remy at once."

"But can't he even see Aunt Titi?" Colette began.

"Yes," I broke in, "I know Vincent would want to see all of us."

"Believe me, Madame," he said, addressing his remarks to Aunt Titi, the adult of the group, "He is in no condition to see anyone. His thoughts are incoherent. I fear another attack is already in progress. The most beneficial course for poor Monsieur Vincent is to return him to Saint Paul de Mausole at once."

And sadly we watched as Trabuc climbed into the carriage and it rolled quickly out of sight. We never saw Vincent at all. And the picture he had brought to give to my aunt. What had happened to it?

CHAPTER TWENTY FOUR

Aunt Titi grew stronger each day and I began to yearn to return to Etienne. The secret I carried was his secret also, and I longed to tell him. Each day I had written, but I was saving the news of a baby until we were together.

These were my thoughts as I performed my old task of readying the cafe for the evening meal. I liked shaking the cloths and spreading them smoothly over the tables, placing the napkins and silverware. It gave me plenty of time for thinking. Colette slipped in quietly as I worked and sat down.

"Feel free to lend a hand," I smiled at her. Aunt was upstairs resting while Joan was probably in our room arranging her hair, a favorite pastime.

"Hubert Lantier has announced his betrothal to Suzette, the girl at the baker's,"

Colette's words burst upon my thoughts.

"There is no accounting for taste, is there?" I joked. "What is the news of Edmond?"

"He is not coming to the cafe as often as he once did. I think he may have found someone else to walk out with." Colette's lower lip was trembling and I was distressed to see large tears form in her eyes.

"Colette, Colette," I said, hurrying to embrace her, "don't fret." What a disaster I thought. I'd advised her to confide in Hubert, thinking he would approach Edmond with the news and bring him speedily into my sister's arms. It had not happened. I felt a *frisson* of fear. Had I made a terrible mistake?

"I am so miserable, Minette. I cannot bear to see him drift away."

"Colette, do not worry. He may feel afraid to declare himself. Some men are very shy and uncertain in that way. Why don't you let him know just a little of your feeling for him. Help him along a little. Try to arrange a few minutes alone when you can speak together. Then tell him how you feel. At least you would know then. What have you got to lose?" Colette agreed reluctantly, but she still looked miserable as she climbed the stairs. My heart was heavy for her.

There was plenty of time to think about Etienne, the baby, and plans for the future as I went on with my work. What would we name him, or her, I thought hastily. It might be a girl. The thought of our own little one made me wish for that moment when I would hold the baby in my arms.

No word had come from Vincent and I feared the worst, that his attack was one of the longer ones. Was he still imprisoned in that horrible twilight world in which the attacks deposited him? It was a world of nightmares, hallucinations too dreadful to contemplate. Every day I prayed that he might recover, and that the enervating disability would leave him and he would at last be at peace to carry on his life's work.

I heard a soft tap on the window and turned around. A smartly dressed woman motioned to me to open the door. Then I recognized her. It was Gisele, but a Gisele changed in appearance almost beyond recognition.

Quickly I moved to let her in, taking note of a new grey bombazine dress of the highest quality, a rich shawl of wool paisley with long fringe. That cost a pretty penny, I thought. On her head was a cunning little slip of a hat, bending over one eye and decorated with an ostrich plume running around the crown. She was wearing beautiful leather gloves and shiny new boots.

Clearly Gisele had experienced an upswing in her fortunes. The eye which looked askance in another direction peered out from under the pretty hat. The skin normally erupting with pimples was disguised somewhat by a filmy dusting of powder. Yes, it was Gisele all right. There was even a little rouge on her lips. She looked almost pretty, I thought.

"Gisele! How smart you look. My goodness, what lovely clothes. Come inside and tell me how you are getting on," I said, my amazement getting the best of me.

"I had to see you, Minette. I had to get this package to your aunt before I left." For the first time, I noticed she carried a slender wrapped rectangle under her arm.

"I see. But surely you are not leaving?"

"Leaving Arles," she answered proudly. "Leaving for good."

"Sit down for a minute," I said quickly as she looked nervously around. I knew she did not want a tongue lashing from Aunt Titi. She looked like a bird poised for flight. Too late we heard footsteps on the stairs and Aunt entered the dining room. Her face was a picture as she peered at the figure before us and recognition dawned.

"Why it is Gisele," she said, amazed.

"Yes, Madame. I hope you don't mind my coming to the cafe. I had to bring this to you." Solemnly she handed over the package. She is bringing her a gift to thank her for the sugared almonds, I thought.

For once Aunt Titi was at a loss for words. The package was of lesser importance than the transformation of this ugly duckling into a person of means. But how had she come by it? My aunt's face reddened and her eyes flashed. The hussy, I could imagine her thoughts, she has sold herself to the devil!

But Aunt tried not to show her displeasure. Politely she accepted the package. I held my breath. "You have waited a long time to come by to see me, Gisele," she said.

"Yes, Madame, I have," Gisele replied calmly. "I knew you

were disappointed in me for leaving here. I did not want to face your disapproval. But now I am about to leave Arles, and, well, I had this package to deliver to you before I left. So I came."

"You shouldn't have . . ." began my aunt but Gisele quickly interrupted.

"Oh, it is not from me, Madame. Someone else gave it to me to give to you."

Aunt and I looked quickly at each other. Aunt Titi undid the string and removed the wrapping. It was a painting by Vincent of almond branches against the sky. It was signed and dated. At first glance I thought, this is a copy of the one he is sending to his young namesake.

It was a beautiful study. The branches with their pale white blossoms stood out against a blue sky. My aunt was greatly moved. In her mind, this was the picture he should have painted instead of the Night Cafe of long ago.

"But Gisele, how did you come by this? Are you sure it is meant for me?"

As Gisele struggled to frame her explanation, I could tell it was hard for her to keep the sequence of events in order, but she was determined to discharge her duty.

"Monsieur Vincent came to the house where I work on the Saturday around noon. He came straight into the kitchen where he knew I would be working. I was helping the cook scrub the vegetables for the dinner in the evening. We have a cold lunch most days at the, ah, house. He wanted to see how I was getting on. He is always kind to me, Monsieur Vincent. I have never known anyone so kind except Saint Francis. I liked him best when I was with the Sisters." She looked at both of us and we nodded. In her mind, the Saint Francis of the chapel altarpiece was a real person.

"Well, he had the package under his arm and he said he did not want to lose it. He said it was for you, Madame, and he would take it to you later. Then he went in to see some of the, ah, hostesses. Two of them, Renee and Jacqueline, decided to play a trick on him. They got him drinking wine when he thought it was watered wine. They offered him glass after glass until he did not even know where he was. Then he fell asleep and slept until around noon of the next day. That would have been a Sunday."

Gisele paused here to assemble her thoughts. Aunt and I realized what a great effort this was for her. Almost too taxing.

"I found out about the rest of it later. You see, I had to go out to the farmer who furnishes us with vegetables because we had run out and there was nothing for the dinner. The farmer had gone to church and I had to dig the potatoes and carrots myself. I was a fright when I finally got back."

"And Monsieur Vincent?" Aunt gently returned her to the subject.

"Well, he was gone, Madame, by the time I got back. They said two men from Saint Remy came in a fine carriage and carried him away. When he awoke earlier, they said he did not know where he was and was raving like a lunatic. Madame Clotilde, the woman I work for, was about ready to call the police when they turned up and took him away."

"Cretins!" Thundered Aunt Titi. "Did they not realize he is a very sick man? Teasing him indeed! They are the ones who should be put in jail!"

"I agree with you, Madame," Gisele spoke up. "Jacqueline and Renee had no right. And Madame, I forgot all about the parcel until I was packing up to leave. You see, I am leaving tomorrow. When I found it in my closet, I knew I had to bring it to you straightaway. I would not want something that is not mine."

"Now, now, Gisele. Do not fret yourself. You have done the right thing. But tell us, why are you leaving? Where are you going?" Aunt's voice was kind.

"It is like a miracle, Madame. Truly it is. There is this farmer from Avignon you see. He comes to, to the place from time to time, the place where I work. He is a kind man and well-to-do yet he is different from most who come there. He, well, he did not want to be with any of the hostesses in that way. What he wanted was to talk with someone. Since I was never with anybody I was called in to talk with him sometimes when all the others were . . . busy." Here Gisele paused again and Aunt and I exchanged glances.

"Then he started asking for me to talk with him first off, before he even inquired about anybody else. We got to be friends and we talked, mostly he talked, about how much he missed his wife, who died. They did not have any children, you see, and he was all alone in the world. Just like me." Here she paused again, her thoughts on herself.

"He is very respected in his community. He always traveled to Arles so nobody would suspect . . . He goes to mass. And he has promised we will go every Sunday! That made me so happy! He accepted me, Madame, for what I am, a poor orphan girl who is very plain, most would say ugly." Here I lowered my eyes. She was not deceived about what people thought of her. It was embarrassing that Gisele was so honest with herself. But her strength showed in her acceptance of the truth.

"He asked me to marry him. He brought me these clothes. He says I can pick others, of my own choice, after we are married. Tomorrow he is coming back to take me to his house in Avignon. First we will stop at the church to be married by the priest. The bans have been posted. It will be right from the moment we step into his house. He and I both feel the same way about that," she finished simply.

Aunt rallied and sent me to the kitchen for coffee. Then we sat around the table offering our congratulations to Gisele. She was right, it did seem like a miracle in some ways. Certainly it was a Cinderella ending for Gisele, in spite of her fall from respectability. She deserves her happiness, I thought, feeling a pang for poor Colette, who was convinced happiness was eluding her.

We watched Gisele as she left the cafe and walked down the street.

"A miracle, surely, Aunt," I said.

"It was the nuns, Minette. The nuns at Montpelier who raised her when she was a child. Their prayers for one of their own have redeemed her."

*   *   *

After Gisele left, Aunt and I examined the painting more closely. I was sure Vincent had painted it out of doors. He had looked up at the blossoms from underneath and had painted what he saw. The blue background was not the wall of a room. It was the sky.

We could tell that blossoms and branches were painted first, then the sky was filled in. The blue of the sky was textured, emphasizing that it was a real sky with all of its variations. I told Aunt that in a letter Vincent had told us he was planning to paint a similar work for his new nephew and namesake. This painting must have been done just recently, at the same time.

"Yes," agreed my aunt, "For the almond trees bloom early in the Midi, late January or early February." She thought the painting was beautiful. She treasured it for the rest of her life.

*   *   *

When I returned to Nimes from Arles I found Etienne had accomplished wonders during my absence. The dirt floors of all the rooms had been completely covered over with tiles. The rooms were taking on a finished look. It would not be long before we could move in.

Etienne's joy at the news of our baby was wonderful to behold. He became quite fussy about the food I ate. He refused to let me do any heavy work. In short, he treated me with very special care. I could see that he was going to be a wonderful father. As for *Maman*, she could not be restrained from knitting and crocheting a plethora of booties and sweaters for her coming grandchild. Etienne teased her saying that the child would turn into a fop, a dandy.

We spent the evenings talking about possible names for the baby, discussing which room would be best for the child after he had outgrown the cradle which would be in our bedroom. The nausea and queasiness of the morning sickness had stopped. I felt better than I had ever felt in my life. Etienne allowed me to help a little with the whitewashing of the walls, but he refused to let me near the ladder.

We had written several letters to Vincent, but had received no reply. Not since we had made the journey to the asylum near Avignon. By late April we were afraid of the worst. Then I received the following brief letter:

> Dear Madame Martin:
>
> I note that several letters have arrived for Monsieur Van Gogh from you and your husband. We are keeping those letters until such a time when he will be able to read them.
>
> En route to Saint Remy from Arles on 23 February he suffered the most severe attack to date and is still slowly recovering. Hopefully he will be well enough so that we may give him the letters soon.
>
> Your obedient servant,
> Trabuc

The letter was dated 22 April.

Two months! Etienne and I were greatly saddened by the news. But I cannot say we were completely surprised.

"I feared something like this had happened," Etienne said.

I immediately thought of the wine-drinking orgy "to tease him" by the empty-headed Renee and Jacqueline and came as close to hating anyone as I have ever done. Poor Vincent. How desolate and abandoned he must feel.

He once expressed the thought in a letter that the climate of Provence was the cause of his attacks. My feeling was that his stay at Saint Paul de Mausole had been nothing but one attack following another. The asylum was responsible, I believed. Everything about Saint Paul de Mausole shouted "neglect." Why couldn't they do something to help Vincent?

CHAPTER TWENTY FIVE

W hen Colette's letter arrived, I realized I had been so absorbed in my pregnancy, my busy life at the farm, that I had pushed her troubles to the back of my mind. It was with feelings of guilt that I began to read.

Dear Minette,

How much I have been wanting to talk with you! Aunt Titi is kindness itself, but she would never understand how I feel, how I still feel about Edmond.

But I get ahead of myself. It took me over a week to bolster my courage enough to decide to tell Edmond of my feelings for him as you suggested I do. He has been unfailingly correct and polite, but somehow distant and appeared very nervous at our last meeting. I had the feeling he was upset, but I determined to go ahead with my plan. Before I could speak, however, he launched into the most amazing account.

A few years back, he had been in love with a girl in his town, a girl of whom his family disapproved. His father sent him, and Hubert, to Arles on the pretext of learning the business from a merchant friend of his father. The real reason was to distance Edmond from the girl. However, they continued to keep up with each other by secret letters.

Minette, the girl had a baby recently, Edmond's baby! At first Edmond lacked the courage to face his father, but when he went home last month for his holiday, he stood up to his father and told him he was going to marry the girl, even if his father disowned him. He told his father about the child, and this softened his heart. He has given them permission to marry and Edmond is leaving Arles.

All of this poured out of him before I said one word, so there were no tearful scenes, thank goodness. I could not have borne that. I am sure however, that Edmond already knew my feelings. Hubert had told him. Never mind, it is over now, and my pride is intact, but oh, how desolate and alone I feel.

Please, Minette, do not blame yourself for this. Nothing could have changed anything. His heart was already given to someone else. I could never have loved Hubert. For me, it was only Edmond. And he was spoken for.

So it seems that I am destined to live a single life! Life is so strange, Minette, if you can laugh through your tears. Take good care of Etienne. Remember, I always said he was your perfect mate. And good men are rare. Please write soon.

Your loving sister,
Colette

Oh my poor, poor sister. Only sixteen and her heart already broken twice. I knew I must answer her letter at once, but what could I say? Only express my love and concern. It was not a solution, but it would help.

As chance would have it, Pierre visited the *cabane* as I was composing the letter. I liked this shy, older version of Etienne. I asked him about Agnes. It had been some time since I had seen them together.

"Agnes and I are no longer going out together," he said. Quickly I looked up from my paper.

"It was never serious with me," he continued. "I was dazzled by Agnes, but when I got to know her better, there was really very little similarity between us. Her beauty just wasn't enough."

"I am sorry, Pierre," I said. "I am fond of you both."

"Don't be sorry. What would have been tragic? A marriage. No, Agnes is fine. She is already seeing someone else. Who are you writing?"

"To my sister, Colette. She too, has just ended an unhappy love affair. It is a difficult letter to write."

"When it is finished, let me take it to her for you. I must go to Arles on farm business tomorrow. I could deliver it to her."

"Why Pierre, how thoughtful of you," I said, and gave him the address of Cafe Ginoux.

Later that night, when I was relating news of the day to Etienne, who already had known of the departure of Agnes from Pierre's life, I remembered the admiring glances Pierre had sent to Colette at our wedding in August.

"Don't jump to any conclusions, Minette," Etienne said sleepily, "Wait and see."

* * *

May 10, Saint Remy
Dear Minette and Etienne,

Once more I have come up from the depths into the world again and I am filled with energy, bursting with enthusiasm for my work again. This last attack has left me shattered.

But first, Etienne, I wish to thank you for your letter to me about the asylum at Montdevergues. I had in my mind all but determined to go there when I leave this place, but my brother kept writing me that I should be nearer to him and his family, that I should move to the North. And as I had written you at an earlier time, I do feel this Southern climate may be responsible, at least in part, for my series of attacks.

So my friends, I have decided I will move to the North. They say blood is thicker than water. Well, my brother has been like a father to me, a kind, loving and supportive father for many years, and I truly believe my place is near him. I know I cannot bear the strain of life in Paris more than a few days. But I will journey north of Paris, to Auvers-sur-Oise, the little village I mentioned before, where a doctor lives who can help me, I hope.

I will live at an inn until I am somewhat settled. If all goes well, perhaps there will be a studio for artists of the North, similar to the Little Yellow House. We will see. At least I will be quite near my brother, his wife, and my little nephew.

It has become crystal clear to me that I must leave this place at once. I have suffered too much. As to whether the Northern climate will be more beneficial to me I cannot say. What I do know is that when I leave the Midi, I will be leaving a part of myself, for I have loved not only its fields, vines, olive trees and cypresses, I have loved its people too.

Doctor Peyron has given his consent for me to leave so I have begun my packing, and so I am near to the end. My plan is to leave on May 16, a Saturday. I am sending my luggage ahead, carrying with me some frames, my easel and stretchers. I am writing Madame Ginoux asking her to hold my furniture a little longer. As soon as I am settled, I will ask her to send it on to Auvers.

The most recent horrible attack has disappeared like a thunderstorm and I am working to give a last stroke of the brush here with a calm and steady enthusiasm. All has not been a disaster at Saint Paul de Mausole. I am working on still lifes—irises and roses. I plan to finish them before I leave, but they will take a whole month to dry. Good Trabuc has offered to send them on to my brother's address when they are ready. It is touching to see how sad he is to see me leave. He is a good man.

Minette and Etienne, when I think of the many things we three have shared, and how always you have extended a helping hand to me, it makes me so sad to go. True friends do not come along often, and it pains me more than I can say to be leaving you. I think you know that I take this step for my very survival. I must have help, and I look to my brother to sustain me. I am fighting for my life, most of all for all the paintings within me still to be created.

Dear Friends, do not feel sad as I leave Provence. Look for me as you feel the hot yellow sun bathing the fields in such wonderful golden light, as you see that same sun setting, turning the vines and the grapes of the vineyard into a sea of red wine, as you look up in wonder at the night sky and reach for stars that outshine the jewels of the most pampered princess.

Au Revoir. I pray we shall meet again.

Vincent.

* * *

That was the last letter we received. I never saw Vincent again.

However, Paris newspapers carried the story of his death, the eccentric Dutch painter, Vincent Van Gogh, who shot himself on 27 July, 1890 in a field outside the village of Auvers-sur-Oise. He died the following Tuesday. He had been in Auvers little more than two months. The newspaper account continued.

The funeral was held on Wednesday. By mid-morning friends of Vincent had begun to gather at the inn of Monsieur Ravoux where he stayed. His brother Theo was said to be inconsolable in his grief. Emile Bernard, Charles Laval, Andries Bongers, A.M.

Lauzet, Pere Tanguy and Lucien Pissarro were among the artists present.

The room where his body lay was filled with flowers—sunflowers, which he loved, and dahlias and other yellow flowers. Around the place where his body lay, his canvases had been nailed to the wall, forming a sort of halo around the coffin. The coffin was spread with a simple white cloth and flowers were massed on top. Near him they placed his easel, his folding stool and his brushes.

At three o'clock his friends raised the coffin and carried it to the hearse. The parish priest had refused to officiate at the funeral because the dead man was a suicide, so the friends walked behind the hearse to the cemetery at the top of the hill and Dr. Gachet, a friend and doctor of the painter, could say only a few words, as he was almost overcome by grief.

"He was an honest man and a great artist. He had only two aims, humanity and art. It was art that he cherished above everything, which will make his name live." So the doctor ended his eulogy.

*   *   *

As it often happens, the world, which had largely ignored Vincent during his lifetime, began beating a path to worship at his feet after he was dead, almost before the flowers on his grave had wilted.

No one, not even Etienne, could know how I really felt when I read the account of Vincent's suicide in the Paris newspaper.

The sound of that revolver echoed over and over again as I imagined Vincent alone in that field, sunk so deep in despair that the only path to release seemed to be a bullet. I could not reconcile his death with the man I had known who loved life with such passion, who saw the world's beauty in such unique and hidden ways.

What drove him to this?

Books in great numbers by learned men have tried to explain

his actions. He was stricken by another sudden attack. His brother had threatened to stop sending him money for his support. The whole thing was a tragic accident. Theories, only theories.

I believe despair over his mental state finally drove Vincent, clearly and logically, to take the action which ended his life. The attacks had become so horrible, so frightening, that he simply could not face a lifetime of such terror. They were unbearable. He had come to the end of the road. And so he decided to end his life.

And when he did it I believe he was rational and logical and determined. How else can it be explained that he prepared himself by obtaining a revolver?

Theo Van Gogh was shattered by grief after his brother's death. As his health steadily declined, he spent all of his time trying to perpetuate his brother's memory. He resigned his post at the art gallery. He became obsessed with carrying out projects he and Vincent had envisioned. But his mental health broke down. He had to be locked up. Slightly improved, he was taken from Paris to Holland by his wife. He died there January 25, 1891, less than six months after Vincent. He was thirty three years old.

Twenty three years later, his wife had his remains transferred from Holland to Auvers and placed beside Vincent. At last, the brothers lie peacefully side by side.

*   *   *

Both Etienne and I were deeply saddened by Vincent's death. As the days went by, we decided on a way to honor our friend whom we both had loved so much. We named our son, born November 21, 1890, Vincent Etienne Martin as a living memorial to Vincent Van Gogh.

He was the first of five healthy sons. Our farm prospered, the *mas* became a comfortable home, filled with the laughter of children. I tried to instill in my children a love of beauty, a love of and respect for nature, and a love of life, some of the most precious legacies I received from my friend Vincent. And I also taught them to revere learning, to be curious of the world around them.

My sister Colette never married. Her friendship with Pierre came to nothing, and she continued to live with my aunt until she died. My mother and brothers made a success of their farm and were able finally to purchase the land on which they worked. My brothers married and the farm is still in the hands of Ginoux descendants.

My dear husband, Etienne, died when he was sixty and I turned the running of the farm over to my sons. I moved to Arles to live with my sister, who operated the Cafe Ginoux until her death fifteen years ago.

Alone now, I have plenty of time to recall the past and my many blessings. And to remember with affection the amazing, brave human being who was my friend, Vincent Van Gogh.

ACKNOWLEDGMENTS

It is the novelist's privilege to make up what she likes, even when real people and places enter the story. Arles in this book is made up of some fact and some fiction, as are Saint Remy, Nimes, and so on. While the cafe existed, along with Vincent's Little Yellow House, both are gone now, the latter finished off by a wartime bomb. Therefore this book mirrors only the writer's state of mind. Vincent Van Gogh, Paul Gauguin and some of the lesser characters, Madame Ginoux, for example, actually existed. But their interaction with fictional characters and with each other is imagined.

I have tried to stay true to the facts of Vincent's art, being greatly helped by his letters to his brother Theo and others in which we are privy to his innermost thoughts about his work. I have read many books on Vincent Van Gogh. Some I liked best include "Van Gogh in Provence and Auvers" by Bogomila Welsh-Ovcharov; "Van Gogh in Arles" and "Van Gogh in St. Remy and Auvers" by Ronald Pickvance; and "Van Gogh, The Passionate Eye" by Pascal Bonafoux. As a general overview of the period, "Post Impressionism from Van Gogh to Gauguin" by John Rewald, remains a classic.

To the many family and friends who have helped me along the

way I am especially grateful: to Daisy Warnalis and Holly Williams, my daughters, to Bill Smith and the Piedmont Writers Group, to Gay Tucker, Joyce Maddux, Marguerite Watkins, Jane Harwood, Agatha Clemente and from afar, Priscilla Tolkien and Annela Twitchin for their encouragement which always arrived when it was most needed. My thanks to Nick Kuckel and Rachel Davey of Xlibris for smoothing the way. Finally, I am indebted to my husband James whose unfailing support made this book a reality.